SCORING DRIVE:

A Journey in a Secret Privileged Society through the Eyes of Coaches

By Ron "Clump" Taylor and Keith "Mac" McKelphin

ISBN: 0-9799927-1-0
ISBN: 978-0-9799927-1-1
LCCN: 2016913351

DEDICATION

We dedicate this book in loving memories of our fathers, for their unconditional love and stewardship. Thanks for always being there for us! You both left an impression that has made us the men we are today. We are honored to continue your lessons and legacy that will never be forgotten. We love you! Continue to rest in peace...

FOREWORD

I have been a part of coaching for over 40 years. What follows is a truly remarkable true to life depiction of what occurs within the ambits of the coaching fraternity, but outside the scrutiny of the mainstream media in this information age. Two young men arrived on campus to varying fanfare, each the center of their respective universes. Not only would they learn to coexist on this smallest of campuses as gifted athletes, but Ron "Clump" Taylor and Keith "Mac" McKelphin would develop the sort of relationship that would transcend time.

What you will find in this novel is that both Clump and Mac have captured the unique journey that so many coaches experience to varying degrees. It's hard to believe this work is fiction because I have experienced the events recounted herein many times in my life. In a straight-forward and hard-hitting way, this novel gives society a view of the hidden world of coaching.

Every coach I know has a friend who took the journey with him/her. This story centers on the friendship between Eric and James, which is neither uncommon nor unique. At times, a coach's friend becomes his/her biggest rival – in life or on the field. This story is no different but serves as a vehicle through which the stories of the young men who would soon see Eric and James as primary and secondary father figures.

I want to thank Clump and Mac because very few people with their insight would dare to openly address the issues of infidelity, alcoholism, racial inequalities, jealousy, and relational dynamics within the coaching world.

This is a remarkable book that I would recommend to anyone thinking about becoming a coach, or anyone who would like to get a small snapshot of what we go through. At first, I thought this would be another cookie-cutter book on how to become a great coach. But in the end, I found myself pulling for these young men, their players, their families, their teams. You will find yourself pulling for them, too.

Eddie G. Robinson, Jr

CONTENT

ACKNOWLEDGEMENTS

We would like to thank our families for understanding and supporting us as we took them through our journeys in coaching. This book is for you!

Special thanks to Broderick Simmons (KS Productions), Jarrett Burgess, Morgan L. Taylor for your knowledge wisdom and expertise in editing our book, and Ron Taylor, II for your artistic expertise with the book cover.

PREFACE

The co-authors of the work you are about to read have been involved in the coaching profession for many years and have been blessed with the privilege to be members of a special secret fraternity that many hope to enter. We have read many books regarding this profession, but we felt it was our time to write a book that shares experiences inside and outside this select fraternity. It appears to be a rite of passage among published authors to produce an autobiography, military books, or even business books, but to the best of our knowledge and diligent research, we have never come across any book regarding the unique road that all coaches travel to reach their dreams of success.

Most people will never understand and know the intricacies of this journey. They will never truly be able to comprehend this journey, nor will they ever believe what the amazing journey holds. We can understand and empathize but ask for and appreciate open minds through this coaching process since many young coaches neither contemplate nor understand what they face.

The two of us have formed a special mentor-student partnership in order to develop an incredible team. With over 40 combined years of experience in shaping young athletes into productive members of society, we have touched many lives. We were involved at several levels of athletics like the Bowl Championship Series, Football Bowl Subdivision, and Football Championship Subdivision (formerly I-AA), Division II, Division III, and professional football. We have touched the minds and hearts of many people. We have spent long hours, much conversation, and many restless nights compiling our experiences and knowledge into a simple yet delightful novel from which others can gain insight.

It is our hope that the readers will embrace this journey as their own. It is an incredible and revealing look at the weaknesses and insecurities of human beings, as well as a look into the secret lives and privileged society of coaches. Through our eyes, you will understand that many coaches will never reach the pinnacle of a BCS conference and find that smaller schools are represented by some of the best and brightest minds ever to coach.

The main characters on this journey, Eric and James, are the compilation of many coaches who have survived this awesome journey. This book takes you from the final college game of two friends and football teammates, all the way through their paths in the cycle of coaching. You will find that not all coaches are born to coach and that some coaches start due to necessity. Unlike Eric and James, thousands of coaches will never complete this exciting, long, and sometimes seemingly unfair journey.

1 TEAMMATE

I remember the day that I arrived on this campus. I committed to Maryland State University following my junior year at Madison. I figured that I'd show up and show out immediately. I was the complete running back, but if it wasn't for my core courses, I would have been playing on the Forty Acres, yeah, the University of Texas. But anyway, State has been good to me, real good! I only need twenty yards today to hit 1,700 yards for the third consecutive year. But all everyone talks about is James. I'm the engine in the car, they're just the rims. I know, people see the rims, and only hear the engine. The story of my life, no recognition.

This will be the last rodeo for twenty-three seniors including myself—John Manning—Eric Fellows, and James Ryan Leaf. Walking around this locker room for the last time, the paint peeling off the walls, pools of water in the corner, tattered seats, rusty showers, how the hell did we stay here? Why? How were we able to play up to our capabilities with these shitty facilities? I've taken four team photos, and I can't remember once seeing them posted here or in the coaches' offices. That stereo system in the middle of the room? Donated by a former player selling insurance in Texas. Needs an upgrade. Who plays cassette tapes anymore these days?

We only have two *real* trainers. The other six are freshman just learning the ropes. I learned to tape my own ankles as a sophomore. Look at them over there kissing Eric's pass dropping ass. How two trainers gonna tend to one player? People around State, alumni, fans, teammates, coaches, all loved Eric because he is perceived as an overachiever. Eric is State's version of "Rudy." Just a hair above a walk-on, but made it work.

I can't complain. It's been this way my entire career. I recognized early on that Coach depended upon me to help the team build a lead, a cushion if you will. From that point, they were free to unleash the Beast—

let him start gun-slinging and running around entertaining the crowd. I always knew that they appeased him that way. I got mine. The scouts see me, just as they see him. I never wanted to be quarterback. Coach offered me a shot heading into spring of my junior year. Please, James would have never gone for that. I wanted no part of it anyway. What little team chemistry we had was centered on James heading the offense with the defense following his lead. I stand 6'2" at 212 pounds. I run a legit 4.5 in full pads. My football journey will most certainly continue.

It was the final home game of the year, and the biggest. The Maryland State University Bisons was playing their rivals from Cumberland State University – a bunch of fucking assholes from the hills of Maryland. The fans are country and classless. They start tailgating on the Wednesday before the game—all over town, in the stadium parking lot, and anyplace you can plug in one of those gargantuan Winnebago's. Cooking out, talking shit, getting drunk, heckling us at practice, this is some bullshit.

Oh, Cum State is what we call them. It's a great pun, but the name primarily centers on the fact that these fans will do anything to help their team win a game, which includes but is not limited to sending some of the hottest ass from Northern Virginia into our dorm prowling with condoms and Hennessey. You know that old rule that coaches always preach: "No sex the night before the game." Bullshit. I ran for 206 and 3 TDs against Arkansas State after having bust two cool ones the night before and a shot of head before the pre-game meal. Trust me, that is some bullshit. So, I love when we play Cum State, home or away, because I know that I'll get my dick wet.

James Leaf, the starting quarterback for State in the Big World Conference, had been "Mr. Everything" during the entire game. He stood only five-foot-nine and excelled at staying in the pocket as a true dropback passer – clearly not very intimidating for a "beast," but a very gifted athlete.

11

He was a beast of a talent. He was coveted as a point guard; To this day, Coach Garrick of the baseball team swears that he had major league talent as a shortstop. He would arrive at the conference meets just in time to anchor both relay teams.

Eric's football career was not as great as The Beast's. He'd been the last football signee for Maryland State University's head coach Jim Charley. The only reason he was signed was because another recruit changed his scholarship commitment and signed with Nebraska at the last minute. During his football career, Eric had played running back, defensive back, and, finally, wide receiver, where he lettered in his senior year as a special teams player. Coach Charley had hoped he would develop into a great football player, but that hope never became a reality. The truth is that Coach Charley stuck it out with Eric because he saw a lot of himself in the young player.

On the day of the last game of both their college years, Eric and James prepared to run out of the tunnel. James leaned over to Eric and said, "Let's go kick some ass for the last time!"

Eric responded, "Yeah it's the last chance to embarrass Cum State. I smell a lot of big plays in the air."

"What you smell is Big Derek, I told him about eating those boiled eggs this morning," says James. The two friends share a laugh.

After all the players ran through the tunnel and got to the sideline, the running back coach, Derek Ray, shouted, "Remember this day!" What they later found out was that game day for a player was totally different than game day for a coach. It ended up being a great game for the Bison. The Beast was at his best, completing pass after pass all over the field, and even Eric had three catches that day.

Despite my best efforts during this final home game, somehow we trailed Cum State by ten heading into the fourth quarter. We got the ball back after Eric forced a fumble with a punishing hit on punt coverage. Eric decleated the ball carrier, separating him from both the ball and his helmet, which shot straight up in the air about eight feet. Eric was generally good for delivering a signature play in his limited playing time. Again, for that effort and the production with limited opportunities, the crowd, coaches, teammates, loved Eric.

Our best play of the game has been a weak-side screen pass out of every one-back set we tried. Surely, Coach would get me the ball. The play is called, but what is Eric doing in the huddle?

We're at the line; I see the same thing James sees. The blitz is coming. I'll chip the linebacker on my way out; this play should go for sixty yards. What the hell is James doing checking off the play? Max protection? I know damn well he's not going to try a post corner to Randall's slow, stone hands having ass. Shit, I gotta cross the formation. I look wide right. There's Eric in the slot with Randall outside. Randall changes the route combo with a hand signal. Now it's a smash route, with Eric to the corner and Randall controlling the boundary corner. James gave a cheap fake to me on his third step and on the fifth step launches a rocket to Eric who still hadn't made it to the top of his route, the free safety is on his ass. Coming out of his break, with his hands up Eric juggles the catch, appears to get a foot down as he gets blown up by the cornerback trying to fall into the route from underneath. The crowd rises to their collective feet awaiting a ruling.

The Side Judge has marked the spot calling it a catch. The Back Judge is giving the "juggling" signal that Eric didn't have control of the ball. Eric is trying to play the role that he made the catch no doubt. But looking in his eyes, he didn't truly believe it. The play took place on the Cum State sideline. But it's Senior Day. Can we get a little homecooking at the last home game we'll ever play at State? The officials huddle. "That wasn't a motherfucking catch!" shouts the Cum State corner. In the weakest voice you could ever imagine coming from a college football player, Eric retorts, "Uh-huh. I caught that. That's a catch all day."

"It has been determined that the receiver had one foot down while maintaining possession of the ball as he was tackled. FIRST DOWN!"

Down ten points, six minutes into the fourth quarter, ball on the Cum State 48. It's "Manning Time!" In the huddle, I all but beg James for the ball. I rushed for 165 in the first half, and then Coach abandoned me. We're down ten, so let's get back to the well before the water runs dry. The play is Slot Right Cross 57 Power O. My play! If I press the hole just enough I can hit the alley setup the safety for a cutback to the right close my eyes and hit my head on the goalpost.

"Green 88! Set!" shouts James signaling the snap, he turns to hand me the ball but stumbles, the center stepped on his foot. Shit, I am already by him without the ball, I turn to look back and James is running for his life. Stiff arms the end, steps out of the diving attempt by the tackle, outruns the Will Linebacker to the edge and scampers thirty yards, just inside the Cum State twenty-yard line.

In the huddle the play came, "Tiger Z Cross 31 G "says James looking me in the eye intently. "JM get this tub and I'll get the next one." I get the pitch, there is penetration front side, I cut back into the inside and get ripped by the Mike backer. Where's the ball? The Cum State fans are going berserk. I am at the bottom of the pile trying to figure out why this was the time to have my first fumble in more than 630 carries. This fumble was especially crushing because all game the defense had hell getting Cum State off the field. Third down conversions KILLED us. On the few times we did stop them, Eric came close to blocking two punts, his specialty. But for the most part, he was neutralized.

This would be a sad day for James, Eric, and the rest of the seniors. For James, he had been a four-year starter, and without a miracle, another season would end without a Bowl game. The final nine minutes of the fourth quarter would feature two long touchdown drives by Cum State. State would answer with an electrifying 86 yard touchdown run by John Manning. For his part, James would launch a 53 yard post pattern to Randall. James finished another drive rushing for another 40 yards on the final drive being tackled at the seven with no time remaining. Final Score, Cum State 41, State U, 31.

The realization of life after State U. had dawned upon James earlier in the final season. Now sitting in the locker room having lost on Senior Day, "The Beast," as James had been nicknamed, alone in front of his locker, began to vocalize that he wouldn't be going into professional football because he was too short by NFL standards.

For James talent notwithstanding, football was his "woman", he loved her, studied her, protected her integrity, espoused her virtues to anyone willing to listen, and knew that there were others who loved her just as deeply. Talent, love for the game, and pragmatic are how James could be best described. He knew his limitations, so he decided to do the next best thing to going pro; He would become a football coach even if it meant becoming a Graduate Assistant with State U.

Sure enough, after his graduation in May, he would come back to State University as a graduate assistant coach. And he wouldn't be alone, either, because his roommate and best friend, Eric Fellows, would also be coaching as a graduate assistant for the defense.

Coach Charley was a big, burly guy with a deep voice reminiscent of *Darth Vader from "Star Wars."* He played his college football at a small Division II football program in Southern Virginia at Bristol Tech College in Bristol, VA. He was a very average athlete, but a very hard worker who gave everything he had while leaving his guts on the football field. He took pride in finding similar prospects to play for him. If a player was a little short or a step slow, he would take a chance because his philosophy was that you can't measure the heart. This tough man mentality was instilled in him as a little kid after his father died. He was the oldest of six siblings. Growing up as the man of the house, Coach Charley delivered papers, cleaned yards, and did anything to help his mom who made money cleaning restrooms at the local motel. To Coach Charley, Eric was the next undertaking of a long line of walk-ons, half scholarships, and one scholarship offer kids upon which he had built State University's sturdy foundation.

Eric and James had become close friends when James visited State on his recruiting trip. Eric, a redshirt freshman at the time, had been his entertainment host. Their bond was solidified the night the hosts took the recruits to Club Shack House, a local spot with a mix of students and locals.

Club Shack House was about ten minutes from campus. Pulling into the parking lot was something to see for James. Eric and James were met in the parking lot by my host, Big Derek and I. James was awestruck. There were so many ladies, so many nice cars, what would the club look like if the parking lot was jumping like this? I had someone hanging on me already. I'm trying to play it cool because I want them all. I'm greedy. James was utterly amazed, country ass.

It was his fourth recruiting trip, but his first to a city as large as Baltimore. He was from a tiny town in western Maryland with a population of 13,000. A town where everybody knew everybody. Like kid in a candy store, it blew James's mind to see how free and friendly everyone seemed. Everyone we passed gave some love to Big Derek and Eric. It was something for me to see heads turn when we entered the place.

****

Big Derek was always one of the cleanest guys on the team. I mean, he dressed as if he owned a department store. Who do you know that's dressed Gucci all the way down to the socks—in college, no less?

As a freshman, I had no idea how Derek came up on such nice threads; however, I did notice that it was a group of seniors who seemed to play with "house money." I would find out later in the semester about the "Outlet Runs."

Twice a month, the seniors would grab a group of freshmen to go out and chase girls at the Outlet Mall. I would discover later that these girls were "ringers"—that is, professional boosters. Big Derek would romanticize the notion of being in a crowded mall and having sex with some of the baddest gals at State. Big Derek took me out one evening, with two other clowns in my class (who would later washout before the second semester).

I was introduced to Candace just as we entered Nordstrom's. Candace was a hot piece of ass, obviously in her early thirties. I didn't pay any attention to her baggy clothes because she showed me some tit and her thong within minutes of meeting me. Big Derek slapped me on the back saying, "Make me proud ... and don't come back empty handed" as he walked in the opposite direction with two exotic women—the brunette had her hand in his pants.

Candace took me into the suit section after a little playful banter and groping. As soon as she looked down and saw that I was aroused, she dove in. Man, if I told you that this was some of the best "brain" I had received up to that point in life it would be an understatement. She was making all those smacking noises looking up at me; people were walking around and I'm trying to keep a straight face. I just knew that security was coming at any minute—because I was about to (you feel me?)

Right in the middle of the session Candace begins to talk to me. She needed my help. She wanted me to promise her. Afterward, she claimed that she would do everything and anything that I wanted. She had some friends that would join in as well, if I was into it. Of course, I promised her the world just as long as I was in her mouth.

Just then, I looked over and saw Big Derek looking my way. He looked at his watch and then gave me the "wrap it up" sign. Candance's iPhone dinged with a text message. She checked the text and didn't miss a beat on that thang. Just then, she said, "C'mon, it's time for that favor."

Candace walked me over to the jewelry section. "Big D says that you're down. I think you're cool, too. We need you to take that bag and run like hell to the opposite exit." I must have looked at this bitch like she was the dumbest broad in America. Just then, she shoved my hand in her pants. "Feel how wet I am, this is all yours. You gotta trust me. Grab that bag and run. You wanna let Derek down? You wanna be a name or the "most known unknown?" said Candace, like she'd said it before. I looked over at Derek. Now it was just him and the rest of the seniors in the group that brought us to the mall. They're eyes said it all. If I didn't grab that bag, I would be labeled a "punk." With no further thought, I grabbed the bag and ran.

I was about ten yards in flight when just about every security guard in Nordstrom's descended on me. I was toast. As they wrestled me to the ground, I turned to see Derek, Candace, and the others walking out with bags in hand. They left me!

I was released three hours later. No charges and no cab fare. As I was walking downtown, lost, Big Derek pulled up with Candace—who was driving an Infiniti G35. He jumped out and told me that I played like a champ. I pushed him off me and squared off. I'm ready to bang. Senior or not, that was a bullshit move. Candace explained that I was the decoy. While the guards were sweating me, they walked away with oodles of goodies. She handed me two hundred dollars. Derek said, "Candace drop me back at campus and take this man to the 'Mo' and bang his brains out. He needs to relax." I wasn't laughing. But the ass was good.
****

While we waited for Eric and Big Derek to get us in, I tried to spot my first conquest through the smoke and strobe lights. James, he had the look of fresh meat, a new boot. Some vixen was sure to eat his ass alive up in here.

For about the first hour, Eric, James, and I just played the wall taking everything in. The music was hot, and lots of girls smiling. Big Derek brought us some beers. In that Texas drawl, he stated, "Yawl bullshitin'! We brought you to the pond where the fish bitin! Drop ya nuts and cast your line, out there! What's wrong yawl scared? I can't play with nobody scared. If you scared to holla at some women WAITING to be hollered at, get your ass back to wherever you from."

After three Coronas and a cup of courage, better known as Grey Goose, James was ready to go in. I was on the floor grinding with a cool piece when James walked out there with the *one* girl I was checking on by the bar. Even without the heels, she was easily six foot. But my boy James was right there trying to make a hand. Her flowing hair had to be weave; it was just too silky with body. She was working that halter top. Although I'm dancing with someone, I am hoping that a tittie pops out. Her skin looked so smooth; I'd be willing to bet she sweats cocoa butter.

Later, I would find out from the Bartender James' friend's name. Before too long, James hooked up with a big, fine, Amazon-looking girl he'd just met in the club that night. Her name was Crystal. Eric noticed that he had not seen this girl around before, but didn't think much of it at the time. Of course, Big Derek knew her, let him tell it. One thing that did catch my eye was Eric and Derek. They was buying the bar—keeping bottles coming. I mean, these are college kids. For a minute, I thought about it. But the Ciroc told me, don't worry about it."

I was just reminded of my recruiting trip to Oklahoma. It's sort of unspoken, but your host gets a stipend, you like that word, stipend? I mean, I did listen in college. Anyway, the hosts get money for each guest. Sort of like a budget. I took a trip to Oklahoma and it was garbage. He mentioned

19

something about not worrying about being a partial qualifier. He said that shit in front of a girl, too, and they just sort of rolled their eyes. I wanted to get in his ass right then and there.

We didn't really do anything—went to some sorority parties. They were tired. The little on-campus so-called hot spots were "butt." The girls were standoffish. But most importantly, I never saw my host coming out of his pocket to take care of me. Oklahoma is Oklahoma. They're recruiting budget is astronomical off-the-top. I can't prove it, but I know that my host at Oklahoma pocketed the money that was meant to be spent on me. Hustle all you want, but don't try to pimp me and definitely don't front on me in front some women.

At that point, grades or not, Oklahoma was out for me.

Alone in the men's room, James told Eric that he planned to have his fun with the girl he'd just met. Ironically, in the restroom, the music being pumped in was Public Enemy's "Rebel without a Pause."

"Man, this bitch is gonna get lucky tonight!"

"Oh yeah?" Eric laughed. "Listen, man, you be careful. And make sure you wrap it up!"

"Yeah, I gonna wrap this conversation up. You saw how she was all over me! I even saw that one fool, the other dude, about 6'3"," replies James.

"You're talking about John Manning, he's a running back. Got some big schools looking at him," says Eric.

"He's too busy checking out my action to enjoy his own," states James, as he hits the door.

As Eric exits, throwing his paper towel in the trash, was that James didn't wash his hands.

Around 2:00 a.m., Big Derek is walking around the club with his shirt all but off, girls under each arm and one climbing his back. "Damn D, you got enough," I said. "Man, John this lil Mexican dude got me for one. I don't remember her name; I just call her "Juan Gone." Anyway, he was cool. I was going home with the older lady; I think she was thirty-two. Her name was Rita and judging by how she kissed, I knew she had to have a helluva head game.

Meanwhile, Crystal told James she was ready to leave. But, this fool ain't driving; he's a recruit like me. I still can't believe that he caught such a tight piece of the cutup. I mean she was fine, but the bitch had a big head. Personally, I can't deal with big head bitches. More power to you, James. I'll take my old lady over some girl that can wear my helmet.

As James was getting ready to walk out with the girl, some white girl was making a scene with Big Derek, while he was just laughing. All I heard was him telling her that *she ruined her own* shirt, something about not swallowing. At that moment, Eric saw the light hit Crystal's face in a certain way, and it gave him pause for a moment. Maybe something wasn't right about Crystal.

He remembered his grandfather telling him once about the knot in people's throats – the Adam's apple – and how you could tell the gender of a person from the size of that knot.

The girl James was leaving with had a large knot in her throat. Oh, shit! Eric had figured it out! Crystal wasn't no dime piece, no honey dip, no redbone, no yellow hammer, no, no, no. Crystal wouldn't be sitting sideways in the Cadillac anytime soon. Crystal was a big faced MAN! She was a man!

Like he'd been shot from a cannon, Eric rushed over to James, but they were in the car and zooming down Montrose Street

21

to points unknown. Eric was frantic. I tried to see about him a little bit, but I had my own fish to fry. Big Derek made sure I was straight and faded me one hundred dollars and three rubbers. He must have pulled them rubbers out his ass because I never saw him go into his pockets or nothing. I looked over to see Eric jumping into his car. Just as soon as he jumped in, he jumped out again and ran back into the club. Whatever, I'm outta here.

Eric would return to his car, reading a note intently. Meanwhile, James and Crystal had arrived at her place. The place was decked out. It was a three-level brownstone in a trendy section of Baltimore just minutes from the marina. James walked in and was awed as if in a museum. There were wonderful works of art—paintings, sculptures, vases. The rugs looked too immaculate to walk-on. While James continued his tour of the house, Crystal prepped and primped to consummate the seduction that began in Club Shack House hours earlier. Following this she walks up behind James, kissing him on his neck. Almost eighteen, he is brimming with excitement *and* anticipation.

Crystal retreats to the kitchen and begins cooking. "What kind of omelet do you want?" Crystal purr was as seductive as it was ominous. "On the real, I just want to put you in the skillet, "replied James grabbing Crystal around the waist and beginning to nibble on her neck.

Eric is now frantic, continuing to refer to his note. Finally, he pulls over to a payphone and makes a call.

James flops on the couch, fumbling with the remote to Crystal's massive television that seemed to appear out of nowhere. Crystal sits on his lap and begins to feed him his omelet. It was arguably the best omelet James had eaten in all his eighteen years.

With each bite he would swallow, Crystal would ratchet up the intensity of her kisses, neck nibbling, lip biting, caressing of nether regions. How many hands does this woman have?

Eric is driving faster now. Just ran his second red light. James' shirt is now off. Crystal is down to her bra and panties tugging at James' zipper. Just as she reaches into his trousers, he is reaching into her Victoria's Secret. Eric makes a quick left and pulls in behind a familiar Lincoln Navigator. Running to the door, Eric begins pounding on it while simultaneously ringing the dog shit out of the doorbell. There's rumbling inside.

James comes to the door in a huff, shirt and shoes in hand. Eric blurts out, "That's a dude!" During the ride back to campus, the only word spoken about the episode was by James.

"Dog, I don't know what happened? Fool cooking eggs, house all decked out, touching on me just the right way, I should've known, dog. And man, I can't believe that I stuck my hands in those panties."

"You didn't …. Did you?" asked Eric.

"Man, that motherfucker packing a Desert Eagle. When you started banging on the door, I put a two piece and pepper on his ass and got the hell up outta there." They give each other a knowing look. Nobody would ever know about this. James' secret would never leave Eric's mouth. From that moment, James had ultimate respect for Eric as a friend and soon-to-be teammate because Eric never rubbed it in his face.

"I guess it's safe to say that neither of us will endure something as embarrassing as that again," said Eric. "You know, there are other things that are worse," replied James.

"Women can be pretty treacherous. You ever wonder why women are called bitches?" Eric had no reply. James answered for him, "it's because no matter how good you treat them, they'll still bite your ass!"

Following the end of the season, there was a shakeup on the coaching staff. Coach Charley was a loving, loyal coach to the point that he held onto a few coaches who just weren't getting it done. Coach Moss was the defensive backs coach and defensive coordinator. His guys rarely broke up any passes; additionally, they might have intercepted ten passes as a unit. Yet, our two corners would be drafted that year—a second rounder and a fifth rounder. Go figure, players with talent, but not much production. Typically, coaching is meant to put talented players in positions to make plays. The odd fact is that Coach Moss LEFT, he was not fired, but chose to coach defensive backs at Kansas State.

There were three other coaching moves made by Coach Charley. Pressure from the Athletic Director was largely responsible for the last three moves. There wasn't as much a call for change because of scheme. It was more of attitude and tone. The coaching staff was collectively advancing in age. The changes were made with a mind to infuse some experience and youth into the staff. Jared Levinthal had been fired from Florida State as defensive coordinator after fifteen years on the staff. Coach Charley hired him to join the staff and meet the experience prong of the Director's directive. As for the youth, that's where Eric and James caught a break.

It isn't unusual for former players to become graduate assistants as opposed to attending graduate school. One day, Eric told James about a conversation he'd had with defensive coordinator Ronald Thompson, who was Eric's immediate supervisor.

"In the past," Thompson had told Eric, "most former players went on to become graduate assistants at other schools where they didn't have any connections with those players. It's easier that way because there's no limit on graduate assistants. Today, you see more players becoming graduate assistants for their former coaches."

What was unusual was that both Eric and James were joining the coaching staff of their alma mater shortly after graduation and coaching on opposite sides of the line of scrimmage. James was part of the offensive staff, and Eric would coach the defensive backs.

The most interesting twist was that during the upcoming spring football camp, Eric and James would be coaching their former teammates now – the same teammates they use to hang out with all around campus and the Greater Baltimore area.

Eric relayed to James that he'd asked Coach Thompson which way was better for graduate assistants of the two which they had previously discussed. Typically, Coach Thompson, an old school coach replied, Coach Thompson was a bit like Coach Boone, played masterfully by Denzel Washington in the movie "Remember the Titans." Thompson had been coaching for over twenty-five years. Eric told James that Thompson had also said it took a special person to do bed check and not frequent the same bars and clubs that the players hung around. James confessed that he wasn't sure that he could report guys with whom he'd fought the enemy on the gridiron.

"You know what? If it means them or me, it's got to be them!" Eric replied loudly, sticking his finger in his friend's face. Eric continued stating, "I'm positive that Coach Charley has someone watching us."

"You don't believe that, do you?" James asked.

"Man, you know Coach Charley is old school and shit. He doesn't quite get all the new ways of doing things. We really have to earn the old man's trust all over again. We're responsible for molding young men into players and citizens now."

The two friends learned quickly that coaching was serious business, and that the State University coaching staff treated it that way. Eric thought he was going to have time to do his graduate course work, socialize with friends, and coach; he soon realized that everything started and ended with football. Everything else in his life was secondary.

A typical day for Eric on the defensive staff started at 7:00 a.m. He had to make sure the film cut-ups being reviewed were set up and ready for the 8:00 a.m. defensive staff meeting, which lasted until 10:00 a.m. Without fail, Coach Thompson always met for the entire two hours. He could take one clip of film and play it back twenty times! At ten o'clock, there was a staff meeting with the head coach, where the old man held court to cover the agenda for the day. Then, at 11:00 a.m., James and Eric would have to go pick up lunch for the other coaches. Nowadays, a lot of coaching staffs have their food catered or delivered. Coach Charley, of course, was old school. Food order and pickup were part of a grad assistant's job, in his opinion.

After lunch, the coaches would break for about hour to work out or to take care of other business. Then they'd return to the office at one o'clock in the afternoon and watch films until 5:00 p.m., when they'd break for dinner. In the summer, 5:00 pm would be the end of the day for the full-time coaches, but not for the graduate assistants. They would have to stay for another two to three hours, breaking down film for the next morning meeting. The two graduate assistants before Eric and James had left after the season to take full-time jobs, and many things that should have been done were left for the two new guys. The old school coaches didn't care to learn about computers or new technology – all they wanted was the final product.

James, on the other hand, had it much easier. The offensive coaches were a very carefree bunch, but they got the job done. Offensive coordinator Fred Davis was very laid back, like he didn't have a worry in the world.

Because he was one of the hottest young coaches in the country, it was only a matter of time before something great happened for Coach Davis. He rarely raised his voice like Coach Thompson did, and he had a calm, smooth confidence about him. He was much younger than Coach Thompson – about thirty-five – and had been coaching for twelve years. He knew exactly what he wanted from his grad assistants and didn't demand nearly as much from James as the defensive staff did from Eric. He also understood technology and did many things for himself. James knew his supervisor's offensive scheme backward and forward, since he had been the starting quarterback and Coach Davis was his quarterback coach. This made it easy because James didn't have to learn any new terminology or techniques.

Though still roommates, things were starting to drastically change between Eric and James. One day, while breaking down film, Eric went into a fit of frustration over James's easy ride as a grad assistant. He told his friend that he was bullshitting every day and not doing half the work Eric had to do.

"Just wait until camp starts," James retorted. "Things will be different."

Eric didn't buy into it. He asked James for help with breaking down film and doing some other everyday duties. Some of Eric's frustration involved his perception of James as not being a great practice player. James seemed to coast on his talent alone in college. Eric felt that James could have worked harder, accepted coaching, and developed his talent. Perhaps James could have given himself a legit shot at the NFL—as a receiver or return guy. Nevertheless, at this moment in Eric's eyes, James' poor work habits were already penetrating into his coaching.

"You're on your own," James replied, and left. James got to go hang out with some girls and drink, while Eric worked. He stayed out much later than Eric ever could. It was a cycle that started to eat at Eric. Each morning as he was leaving for the office, James was either just coming in or snoring in the bed without a care in the world. It was as if James was still a college *junior*. Instead of skipping workouts, treatment, and study hall James was now skipping video prep session, blowing off graduate classes, and failing to prepare for staff meetings. Eric knew better than to attempt to mimic James' behavior. Based upon his career exploits, James had plenty of "good will capital" to burn through before he would find himself in any trouble.

Eric began to wonder if he could make it with all the work he had to do. Since camp and school hadn't started, he couldn't see the light at the end of the tunnel. He wondered when he would get to start talking and learning football. He'd usually just sit and listen as the other staff talked about football. He felt like a gofer, not a coach. No one had ever told him that being a graduate assistant would be so tough.

The tension between Eric and James finally came to a head the weekend before fall camp started. Eric walked into their apartment after a long day, and there was James with a small entourage, getting his groove on one last time before camp kicked off. Eric went ballistic. "Get the fuck out!" was all he could scream at the party guests. "Get the fuck out!" James grabbed Eric and led him outside, where they got into a shoving match. James dared Eric to swing on him. "Eric, boy I will take all the paint off these walls and stairs with your ass. Now, you need to settle down." Eric replied, "I'm just sick of your bullshit." The altercation wasn't about the party, but about the jealousy Eric felt because James was getting an easy ride through a long, hard journey.

Training camp turned out to be another story; both James and Eric had to deal with a new situation where time management was the key. They both got roughly five hours of sleep per night. It was nothing like being a player. Players got the chance to sneak in a short nap. From 5:00 a.m. until midnight, James and Eric were both immersed in their duties as grad assistants. There was just so much to do. Perhaps it was more of a rite of passage, James and Eric were paying their dues to become members of a privileged, elite fraternity—college coaches. It became clear why some teams would have ten grad assistants on a staff in the old days.

The young coaches had become much too busy to continue their feud. They split up their living arrangements and came to learn that conflicts were not uncommon on a coaching staff because egos and pride got in the way. In time, they would laugh about their disagreements. All they had was each other, and their relationship would have to sustain them in the long seasons ahead. These were the biggest lessons for young coaches to learn – how to give and take with each other, and also that coaches see things through their own eyes. They had to reevaluate their friendship and move forward, because coaching and having a working relationship was much different from being teammates.

Once camp ended and the football season started, everything became a blur for them. Everybody had huge expectations for James and Eric, and wanted their requests fulfilled immediately. Coach Fellows and Coach Johnson started to realize that it wasn't about how much football they knew, but about who would make the necessary commitment and sacrifices to become a coach. The next stage in their journey to becoming real football coaches – learning to teach and guide players – was soon to follow.

2 DREAMS

Everybody has a dream. For young coaches like Eric and James, the dream was to one day become head coaches. Thousands of times, the two had said to one another, "When I get my head coaching job …" yet neither had ever really coached. They were both ambitious, but naïve. As seniors, they felt like they knew as much or more about football than Coach Charley and his staff. In five years, Eric had watched thousands of hours of video, had taken volumes of notes. James watched just enough video to figure out what teams were trying to do. From that point, he moved on. James' favorite refrain was, "It's just football, not nuclear fusion." Everyone would laugh because we all knew that James knew nothing about nuclear fusion. In short, they'd never had to guide players in any type of game situation. So, what would they know about running the entire show as head coaches?

Eric was the first to decide that he wanted to be a professional coach. Eric knew early. It was suggested to him by his coaches in high school, athletic trainers at State U. Therefore, by the end of this redshirt freshman year, he was preparing to become a coach. Eric knew the despair felt by college players who'd never made it big, and he knew that they were always looking for some sort of release. Coaching was what most of these players used to get the feeling of failure out of their system, but some never let the feeling go.

During his junior year, Eric had firmly decided to become a coach after realizing that he was always the one who lined up the wide receivers on the field and gave them their assignments. All the wide receivers relied on Eric to do this, because he could explain it in a way that wide receiver coach, Thames Keys couldn't. The wide receivers easily understood him. Eric understood that he couldn't do the things that the receiving unit – Randall, Steve, Mike, Jessie, and Cooper – could do, but this wasn't for lack of trying.

State U was mired in mediocrity. The roster was loaded with decent skill players. The most explosive running back was John Manning, and as much he could, Coach Charley made sure to feed him the rock. Eric knew college football was built on its skilled athletes. State didn't have many. There were two players that were threats to score each time they touched the ball—James and John, that was it. Eric had always questioned why James was not moved to wideout, especially with Robert McIntosh behind him—standing 6' foot 5", weighing 260 pounds, a lefty from Ruston, LA. We called him Hefty Lefty. Incidentally, McIntosh left to focus on baseball becoming a first-round pick for the Houston Astros following his Junior Season. While we were stumbling through the season, Robert was debuting against the Cubs with a three-hit shutout. Now all the players call him "Lucky Lefty."

Eric's coaching philosophy was developing early. He would always seek out great skill players. These were the people who could make opponents miss tackles and make their teammates better players. Wide receivers that could be playmakers were in high demand by colleges, but the possession-type receivers weren't.

Eric didn't tell anyone what he was feeling inside. All he had ever talked about was becoming a lawyer, and he didn't want the embarrassment of looking like a nerd. Nobody envisions a coach sleeping on a mattress in his office four nights a week and thinks, "yeah, that's something that I want to do." But Eric understood and respected that level of personal investment by his coaches. Once he did decide to tell someone, it was James. He and his friend sat up for hours talking about the negatives and positives of his change in career paths, and how his parents would take the news of Eric deciding to become a football coach instead of a lawyer.

"My parents are the ones who have this dream of me becoming a lawyer," Eric said. James interjected, "My parents, I don't know what they wanted me to be. They split up when I was young." Eric replied, "I never

31

knew that. We should talk more about your family, though. Now, enough about you, back to me!" Eric and James laughed hard on that one. Eric continued, "Anyway, I know what I want to be, and that's a football coach. Coaching has been staring me in the face since I've been at State." He took a thoughtful pause. "I'm meant to be a coach. I have to explain everything to the receivers anyway. Coach Keys is too busy talking about bullshit, chasing coeds, drinking, and partying—enough already go back to college or something-- AND the receivers can't even get lined up correctly. Why not get paid, since I'm doing the job anyway?" James defended Coach Keys. He identified with Coach Keys' womanizing. "Don't talk about Coach Keys, he's just doing his thing," said James. Eric just blew off that comment and kept steamrolling with his vision—but what would his parents say?

When Eric told his parents what he wanted to do for the rest of his life, they were a little uneasy but supportive. Shortly thereafter, Eric went to visit with Coach Charley. The two of them had a special bond. The old man knew Eric's football career didn't turn out favorably, but their relationship was still strong. They could talk and relate to one another in a way nobody else on the team could.

Coach Charley asked Eric to say what was on his mind during the team meeting. Eric thought about what to say. When he spoke at the meeting, he talked about how much respect he had for the head coach, and what his help had meant to Eric's life. He told everyone at the meeting how he appreciated Coach Charley, and that he hoped to have this same kind of influence on people's lives.

Afterward, Eric asked Coach Charley, "What would I have to do to become a coach? Would I make a good football coach?"

The old man had been asked these kinds of questions all the time by players and coaches wanting to make it big. Yet, for some reason, Eric asking him these questions caught him by surprise. He said, "Coaching is a wonderful profession and it is very rewarding. I know in my heart that you will make a great coach someday if you apply the same energy you do in practice. I'm not going to tell you how to get into coaching until you think long and hard about the positives and negatives. I want you to put it on paper and report back to me in one week. After that, let's huddle up and we'll move to the next phase."

Coach Charley had never had anyone do this type of assignment before. Why me? Eric wondered. Maybe the coach saw a greater good in Eric that could be given to society. He started second-guessing himself, thinking maybe he wasn't good enough to be a coach since he had to do an assignment. This was unusual because self-doubt hardly ever crossed his mind when it came to football.

Finally, he got around to working on his assignment for Coach Charley. First, he wrote down the positives of coaching. He wrote about helping young people, about teaching and communicating, and about his love and passion for the game. In total, Eric came up with thirty-five positives. The last of the thirty-five positives was good pay. Next, Eric wrote down the negatives. The first negative was the frequent travel. This was followed by the lack of job security and the fact that being a coach was time-consuming. He only came up with nine negative points. Eric finished his list for the night and went to sleep.

The next day, he took his list into James' room to discuss it. James listened to the positives and negatives on his friend's list, and then asked two questions: "If I don't give you the answer you want to hear, will that change your mind about coaching?" and "Do you think coaching will make you happy?"

Eric first answered the second question first, saying that coaching would make him happier than being a lawyer. Then he answered the other question: "If you don't give me positive feedback, I think that'll drive me even more to become a coach, and prove others wrong who doubted me."

"You've answered it for me, man," James replied. "You need to follow your dreams, but remember that dreams don't put food on the table."

What James didn't tell Eric was that all this talk about becoming a coach had started to sway his own future. James had known for some time that he wasn't going to be a professional quarterback. The NFL scouts never brought up his name when they came to the campus—they did mention me, John Manning, but anyway. James wanted to take his college fame and become a businessperson. He was majoring in Business, with plans to start his own little music company but, since all this coaching talk with Eric, he started to have second thoughts about his career choice. James, like Eric, didn't tell anyone what he was thinking. He had a different approach to becoming a coach than Eric did. His plan was to sit back and see how the staff treated Eric as a coach, and then measure this move versus the business move. Eric never knew that he was James' guinea pig, but he was just that, a test subject.

The next day, Eric had to report back to Coach Charley. He walked into his coach's front office and spoke with Alice, the secretary. "Is Coach in?"

"Yes, Eric, he's been expecting you," Alice replied. "I hope you're having a great day today!" As Eric walked into Coach's office, he glanced back to take another look at Alice. Alice was very attractive, old ass people like Coach Charley would say that she "had nice flanks." We would say that Alice was a "MILF." I don't know how many times I went to see Coach Charley and while he was lecturing me about responsibilities, not signing with agents, the perils of unprotected sex—all I could think about was blowing Alice's back out. But I digress. The truth of the matter, Alice was about 50 years old with a body shaped like a Coke bottle. Eric could only image what

Alice looked like when she started working in the football office 25 years ago. James spoke of Alice often since she was tutoring him in a Marketing class. Eric also imaged some of the good, the bad, and the ugly stories Alice must've heard about the coaches who had come through State.

When Eric walked into the office, Coach Charley looked at him seriously and said, "I know you have the list for me. Take a seat and let me look it over." The first thing that hit him was that there were only nine negatives versus thirty-five positives on the list. He didn't say anything for the moment. Finally, he broke his silence, saying, "It seems to me that your mind is already made up about this coaching thing."

"Why do you say that, Coach?" Eric asked, smiling.

"If all you can come up with was nine negatives, then your mind is made up. And I can tell you this – you can be the best coach in the country if you work at it." This, coming from Coach, was the highest praise Eric could get. He didn't make statements like that too often to anyone, in private or in public.

Eric asked the old man if it was possible for him to become a graduate assistant coach at State University. He knew that after the season ended, one of the graduate assistants might be leaving. Coach Charley didn't say much. Being so old school, he preferred for his grad assistants to come from other schools. But in the last few years, he'd started to reconsider allowing his former players be assistants for him. Eric hoped to be next. The coach looked at Eric and said, "Let me talk to the staff about this, and I'll get back with you."

Eric was elated about the way things had gone with Coach, and couldn't wait to tell Angela, his girlfriend, as well as James. He knew they would be happy for him because all he'd talked about was becoming a coach. Both James and Angela were at the apartment when he got there. Angela was a bit flustered, surprised to see Eric at this time of day. Eric shared with them his conversation with Coach Charley about becoming a grad assistant. Neither could believe it. Angela seemed happiest because she was a sophomore, and this would keep Eric close to her for two more years. James was happy as well, and now he knew that there was a chance for him since Coach Charley had so overwhelmingly supported an overachiever like Eric. Overjoyed, Eric told his two favorite people that drinks would be on him that night.

After finding out how well things had gone for Eric, James put his own plan to work. He began stopping by the coaches' offices frequently. He started sitting down to talk football with Coach Davis. He didn't come out and say he wanted to be a coach, but he showed the coaches that he was interested in football more and more. It became a regular occurrence for him to be in one of the offensive coaches' offices. Mind you, throughout his college career James spent a minimal amount of time in the Coaches offices, the meeting rooms, rarely reviewed the video cutups provided on DVD. James did just enough to get by because for the most part his talent always saved him and the team. McIntosh had all the tools, but James had the intangibles. Only Alice would call James on this fact. "You've spent more time in these offices the last few months than during your entire playing Career," she would often say.

One day, unexpectedly, his big break came. Coach Ray, running back coach, asked if James had ever thought about coaching. James looked at Coach Ray and shrugged. "Not really."

"You should," Coach Ray said, looking James in the eye, "you would be good at it." James continued the "ah, shucks" routine which allowed Coach Ray more opportunity to explain the aspects of James' character and personality which would make him a good coach. James always loved having his ego stroked and this occasion was no different. James replied at the end of Coach Ray's presentation, "If you say so, Coach; but, I am really trying to focus on this music thing."

Eric often wondered why James was so into music. One night after some drinks Eric asked him about it. After being quiet for some time, James opened up a bit. "Really, man, I like music, but I don't love it. Truth is, this is just an avenue to get as many women as I can." "You can't be serious, dude," said Eric. But James was truly serious. "After I saw Denzel Washington run those girls in Mo' Betta Blues, I was never the same." Eric couldn't believe that the basis for James' womanizing persona was a movie. James simply didn't strike you as someone shallow like that. James shrugged at Eric's suggestion and returned to his drink, dropping the conversation.

On another occasion, during one of James' visits to the offices, Coach Ray, and Coach Davis both hinted to James that he would make a good coach. It was obvious that Coach Ray had been talking to Coach Davis about James and coaching. I mean these guys were like a pair of bookends. This occasion was different because they—mostly Coach Davis-- said James should think about becoming a graduate assistant. This was a huge step because for the most part James academic career at State U had been marked with changes in major, three semesters of listing his major as undecided, and so on. All the coaches knew that James wanted to play in the NFL, but he wanted to be a quarterback. Thus, James had been so indecisive during his four years on campus, Coach Davis and others wanted James to know that he could decide on what he wanted to do in life—if that decision included coaching, then they would be there to help him. James had his opening into the coaching business.

"Could you help me to get one of those grad assistant positions?"

"I know we are losing one of our assistants," Coach Davis replied. "I think Coach has someone in mind for that one, but don't be surprised if we lose both our assistants, maybe to other schools." Coach Ray gave a nod of approval and essentially confirmation that another grad assistant position would come open.

"Thanks," James said, speculating that Eric would probably get the position.

When Eric finally got confirmation that he was going to be the next defensive grad assistant coach, he was relieved. After all, he had been working at this goal for almost a year. For a long time, Coach Charley wouldn't confirm or deny that he had the job. But now his wait was over. Eric also found out that the offensive graduate assistant was leaving to take a job in South Carolina. This was his chance to ask Coach Charley about the offensive assistant spot, where he felt he would be more comfortable. Eric was certainly always assertive. This was one quality which his teammates respected about him. If there was an opportunity to play, from running back to deep snapper, Eric was in the mix. Now that there was an opportunity to get on with the offense, he wanted it badly.

Eric went to visit with the old man about the position with the offensive side. He got straight to the point but was hit with some surprising news. The position had already been filled by James! Eric couldn't believe this! Yep, James had "backdoored" ole Eric. One would think that it would be some shit about this. But for Eric, it was just more motivation. His best friend would surely have mentioned something like this to him. He was shocked, but in a good way. Now he would have his friend with him, and they could both dream about how they would change the coaching profession for the better while positively impacting the lives of young boys and be instrumental in the molding of young men

When Eric returned home, James was ready to tell him his news. "I have a surprise for you that you won't believe," James said.

Flippantly, Eric responded, "What?"

"I'm going to stay here with you," James began. "Coach Davis told me about the offensive graduate assistant job coming open and asked if I would be interested. I said sure." James continued sounding thrilled, "And Coach

Davis talked to Coach Charley. And that was it!" James had an interesting take on his business aspirations and stated to Eric that "I don't really know if I'm ready for the business world yet. This coaching opportunity will buy me some more time. Man, I'm so excited! Hey, drinks are on me tonight!"

Eric was excited for James, but he couldn't help but wonder why it had been so easy for The Beast to not only make the decision to get into coaching, but Eric was fascinated with how fast James had actually stepped into the ranks. Eric's route was diametrically different and more difficult. Eric decided to chalk it all up to James's "star power."

3 LIVELIHOOD

The season ended on November 13, and this was the second straight season that the Bison did not go to a Bowl game. The flame under Coach Charley's office chair is rising. The alumni are becoming antsy. The student body is finding other things to do on Saturday afternoons. The boosters are squeezing their pocketbooks. The sponsors are looking to the basketball team for better allocation of advertising dollars. Times are tough in the program. It was a rough, injury-plagued year with a very young team, led by a freshman quarterback, but the Bison finished the year with four straight wins for a 6-5 record. It was still disappointing, but the staff and players could envision a brighter future. Without game plans or game meetings, the coaches began to focus their full attention on recruiting. Coach Charley believed once the kids got on campus, with excellent development, that a program could recruit its way out of a malaise.

The six years prior to the Beast's arrival, State was a perennial power in the region and a fixture during bowl season. When the Beast signed, everyone assumed it would be more of the same. What Coach Charley remembered is that all the coaching in the world can't replace talent. "State needs more great players," said Coach Charley to the staff. Continuing, "we are gonna spend a little more money this year. Get out there and find us something to work with. I'm sick of the mediocrity bullshit. Get up off your asses, find us some boys, and call me in when you're ready to close 'em. It's nut-cutting time right now. We'll all be bagging groceries this time next year if we don't turn this thing around." The mood was somber in the room, but the message was clear. Get it done or get out.

Recruiting was meat and potatoes for college football coaches, as they tried to bring the country's best football players to their campuses. During recruiting season, there was always a coach back in the office handling the phones, sending out letters, or making visit arrangements. The NCAA only allowed seven coaches on the road at any one time.

As the season ended, James and Eric entered Phase Two of being graduate assistants. This phase required the handling of tedious day-to-day operations in the office for both sides – work as mundane as searching for a phone number on a coach's cluttered desk. They also had to have the film cut-ups ready for the spring football clinic before spring practice started.

James and Eric could care less about any of their responsibilities. For months, James and Eric had talked about the convention while they listened to the coaching staffs chat and boast about it. They were intrigued by all the talk. Their minds were in another place. Since becoming grad-assistants, they had heard about something going on in January. They were constantly talking amongst themselves and quietly wondering about the big event happening in January. It was the annual World Football Coaches Association Convention to be held in Chicago, IL at the United Center—the house that Michael Jeffery Jordan built. The convention was a massive networking opportunity, where over five thousand coaches of four-year colleges, junior colleges, high schools, and the National Football League would meet to swap ideas, secretly interview for jobs, and do the male bonding thing. It was a coach's annual rite of passage. James and Eric were anxious to get in on that action.

James began spending more time talking with offensive line coach Kenneth Jennings about the convention. James took to Coach Jennings because he was the youngest coach on the staff, only twenty-six years old. Jennings was an All-American offensive guard during his college days. Coach Jennings enjoyed an injury-riddled two-year stint in the League with the Atlanta Falcons. Prior to his employment with State University, Jennings had spent a year as a graduate assistant. James felt the coach could give him credible insight regarding the convention and its activities since he had just finished the grad assistant process.

"Is the convention really fun?" James asked.

"For some coaches – very few – it's lots of fun," Coach Jennings replied, "It's fun for those coaches who have jobs and feel secure where they are. For most coaches, young and old, it's the ultimate meat market. It's about all these coaches trying to sell themselves to the next rung on the ladder. That's what a lot of people really don't know." Coach Jennings would go on to relate to James why a recently FIRED head coach or a head coach with an abysmal record with an also-ran could get hired by a comparable school within weeks. The result was in part due to the relationships forged during these conventions over the years. How does a guy who loses twenty-five games in three years at San Jose Tech get hired as head coach of Michigan?

"Was it hard for you to get a job at the convention?" asked James.

"It wasn't as hard for me because I knew so many coaches who'd tried to recruit me out of high school. Yet, it was still hard trying to inform these coaches that I was now coaching, and that I would do a great job for them as a coach."

James was puzzled because he was not highly recruited—nationally-- out of high school, and now felt some doubt about coaching. He asked Jennings another question: "What about Eric and me? How should we approach the convention?"

"It's interesting that you ask about Eric as well. You may find that there are no friends in coaching for the most part. I mean, you form bonds, but ultimately, you're both trying to feed and provide for your families—or future families. This convention is a business trip. Approach it as such, thinking about you and your family. This isn't college where you can float through taking courses with your buddies." Coach Jennings said. "You should dress nice, be professional, and for damn sure don't drink around coaches you don't know!"

James, like a big dumb kid, asked, "What if somebody offers a drink?"

Coach Jennings repeated, "Don't drink around coaches you don't know! It's amazing, some coaches act like women trying to get attention at a club. Sit back and observe all the fools who drink and act crazy, trying to impress coaches who they believe will help them get a job!" James resolved in his mind that he didn't want to be that guy.

The convention had finally arrived. The State University coaching staff was waiting to grab their luggage at O'Hare International Airport when Coach Charley told everyone to come to his suite for a short meeting once they got checked into the hotel. After making this announcement, the old man departed with his wife to get a rental car. He and Coach Thompson were the only coaches accompanied by their wives. Eric and James figured this was because those two were the elders of the staff.

After everyone had checked into the hotel, they all convened in Coach Charley's suite. He told them all to make sure they carried themselves in a professional manner at all times and to make sure they kept in contact with their visiting recruits since there was going to be a big recruiting weekend once they returned from the convention. Before they all left the room the old man reiterated, "Again, men, make sure you represent and handle yourself appropriately! ACT … LIKE … YOU'VE … GOT … SOME …. SENSE."

Eric and James had made it to the convention but were still full of questions. Before they could make it back to their room, they stopped Coach Ray to ask him why Coach Charley was so stern and cautious. Coach Ray, the second longest-tenured coach on the staff, answered by telling a story about a past convention incident.

"When Coach Charley first joined the staff at State University, during his very first convention, there was a coach on the staff named Rick Mickens," Ray began. "Rick was a great guy, but he wasn't disciplined enough to control himself most of the time. He was on the staff for a year prior to me. Coach Charley really liked Rick, but one night at the convention in

43

Orlando, Rick got with some of his up and coming coaching buddies, and they started drinking. The buddies ended up making it to the neighborhood strip club.

"Damn, the old man tripping off going to the strip club?" asked an incredulous Eric.

Coach Ray continued, "That wasn't the bad part because Coach Charley could have lived with this. But, as the story goes, Coach Mickens left the club with three strippers and took them to his hotel room. What you don't understand is that Rick had his basic room and a two bedroom suite like Coach Charley."

"That's a man after my own heart," said James. Eric began to realize that Rick had planned whatever Coach Ray was about to tell them.

Coach Ray informed the young GAs that Coach Mickens set up shop in his room and started charging admission at the door! It was literally off the hook. As word spread, it became hard to control. Coach Mickens charged fifty dollars at the door. Once the coaches paid, everything else was free. In addition to the three strippers, Rick brought one of the female bartenders to mix drinks. Well, she was basically watering them down for max effect. Most of the coaches were hammered before they arrived.

Mickens had it happening! Drinks were being served in the living room where the stripping was transpiring. The three girls rotated. One stripped while the other two had a room to do private shows, have sex, whatever. Room service kept the food coming with Rick placing $100 tax on each order. This allowed him to pay the room service in cash and not have it charged to his room. Rick kept all the door and food money. He split the stripping and hoe-money with the girls 50/50. He cleared over $7,000 dollars that night. The crowd got so large and rowdy in his room that someone reported the commotion to the front desk.

Eric could see the wheels turning in James' mind as Coach Ray continued to talk. Whenever James was silent and reflexive, Eric knew that James was plotting to go against the grain. Eric had seen that look in James' eye many times during practice and in games right before he would freelance on a play-call. Eric asked, "Coach Ray, with all that commotion, why didn't you guys go check it out and try to..."

"To what? I did go up there. Shit Eric, Rick got a $150 outta me, too. And I've been married for eight years." None of the coaches, even Coach Charley, knew that Rick was raised by his grandparents in Winter Park, FL. The strippers were old classmates from middle school. They were looking to make some money and Rick knew the location of some whales. This was a recipe for money-making and a formula for the embarrassment of the State U football program. Rick's mantra that night was "let the dollars drop and watch those asses POP!"

"Anytime you have this big a gathering of coaches, you know people are going to talk. Mickens Club, as we now refer to this incident, somehow got back to the old man and he went crazy! He fired Mickens for this lack of judgment. Anything could have happened that night! One of those young women could have cried rape or something! Since that incident, Coach Charley has always been on edge about conventions. He wants his staff to enjoy themselves, but in moderation."

Eric and James looked at each other in amazement. They couldn't envision a big-time coach who was making six figures doing something crazy like that. Then again, this story did make it clear why the coaches did not invite their wives to the convention.

As they got onto the elevator that next morning, there stood Grambling State University's legendary coach, Eddie Robinson, talking to another coach from the University of Southwest California. James spoke to both of them. As Robinson replied, asking their names and where they coached, Eric froze. James replied, "We coach at State University. My name is James Ryan Leaf, and this is Eric Fellows."

"I know you like working with Coach Charley," Robinson said. Hearing the familiar voice of Coach Rob gave the Beast goose bumps. Seeing the man that he'd watched on ESPN and on NBC for every Thanksgiving that he could remember was awe inspiring. "Coach Charley and I have been friends for over thirty years. Be sure to tell him hello for me." Eric and James looked like two school kids with big shit-eating grins on their faces. "We will, and go git Southern this year," stated Eric extending his hand as they exited the elevator. James didn't want to leave the elevator. He had so many questions about life, football, women, business, recruiting, and racism—why Coach Rob never left Grambling. Coach Rob saw the eagerness in his eyes. With a pat on the shoulder, "I know son, you come find me and we'll talk."

The two young coaches got off the elevator and headed toward the lobby. The lobby was what they heard about most in all the talk of the convention, and now they were there! Their heads swiveled as they looked all around them at the mad house. Everybody was screaming and yelling to get their point across to the person next to them. James and Eric did the customary walk through and around the lobby. To their surprise, they knew several coaches.

They headed to the vendor exhibit hall next. If a vendor had anything to do with sports, they were there. Anything from energy drinks and energy bars to electronics, footballs, equipment and more – it was all for sale. These vendors didn't care that Eric and James were only grad assistants. They were there to sell their product to whomever or whatever came by. This hall was arguably similar in size and scale to the Consumer Electronics Show held in Las Vegas each year.

"Wow, this place is crazy!" Eric exclaimed. "We're getting to see all these coaches, and we have yet to attend our first lecture." Eric was actively looking for a coaching job but didn't reveal this to James. Eric had compiled a detailed report of his duties as a State U. G.A. and cross-referenced those with the duties of most first-year coaches from a vast cross-section of the nation's major universities. He was ready. James was just glad to be here.

The two friends headed to their first lecture. Eric and James were just two guys heading in the same direction but taking divergent paths. The speaker was Coach Robert Hays, the offensive coordinator at Cumberland State. Eric and James knew they were going to get the dirt on the Bison's biggest rival. They were prepared to report everything they heard to their staff since none of them were in attendance. They thought maybe the staff didn't know. Coach Hays spent an hour discussing how they huddled up, the quarterback cadence, and their one-base formation.

Eric and James realized that the State U. staff probably just knew better than to come to this lecture. They wanted to leave, but sat there with thousands of coaches, dumbfounded. Except for Eric and James, the State U staff had insight that the lecture would be generic or as some would say, "dirtless". They left the lecture and went to hear the defensive coordinator at Capital State College speak on defensive schemes. The coach showed a film covering a pursuit drill that it seemed everyone in the country performed on a daily basis, but Eric and James felt much more connected with him.

Afterward, they went to lunch. They found most of the big-name coaches hanging out drinking cocktails. This was at 11:00 a.m., and it was readily apparent that these coaches were on their third, maybe fourth, round of drinks. Eric and James imagined that all five thousand coaches would be running around, hustling to hear each coach speak, but what they saw was just the opposite. These coaches could care less! This was a free trip to hang out with buddies, chase women, and maybe get a better job. James was with chasing women. Eric used to cringe each time that he heard James say, "Man, a bitch ain't shit!" James would say it anywhere. He would say it around

Angela, at practice, in class, on the bus, in the hotel. James didn't bar 'nan woman. Eric couldn't take it. "James, for a man that gets as much sex as you, why is it that you appear to hate women?" James would briefly explain that he doesn't hate women, he just doesn't respect them. As such, he does what he wants to them with no regard to how they feel about it.

The two made their way back to the lobby after lunch, trying to meet other coaches. They noticed all the young coaches walking around, passing out resumes and business cards. Eric and James were about to do the same thing, but Coach Ray stopped them. He told them this tactic only annoyed coaches.

"They won't hire you or even remember you if you do that!" Coach Ray advised. Eric was crushed. All the hours he spent in front of his laptop and at FedEx Kinkos was for nothing. Coach Ray hammered his two young GAs, "Find a way to get into a conversation, or get someone on our staff to introduce you." All the rest was just bush league. James told Eric, "I'm glad he caught us early. I've never felt better about being 'checked'."

They took Ray's advice and walked over to the job board. It had jobs posted, but only for very small schools that didn't pay very well. It was mostly just full of resumes and cards. "Other than Coach Ray, we haven't seen anyone from our staff yet," Eric commented. "They must be hiding."

Later that day, the two friends bumped into the offensive line coach, Coach Jennings`, who invited them to join him at the presentation of Dr. Tom Osborne, a giant in the coaching profession. The presentation title was "The Nebraska Football Way." The three coaches found seats in the large banquet room where Coach Osborne had already started his speech. His speech astonished them. The speech dealt with community involvement of everyone in the program, even the secretaries. Coach Osborne topics involved a range of activities, from the Susan G. Koman Race for the Cure to Habitat for Humanities. James and Eric could hardly recall (James from memory, Eric from detailed lecture notes) whether Coach Osborne spoke about football. Instead, Coach Osborne focused on building strong, disciplined, young men to enter the workforce after college. This presentation was akin to a sermon. The Nebraska Football Way characterized coaches as shepherds and recruits were the sheep. Performance on the field will take care of itself, but the ultimate job for a coach was to help a young kid in the critical four to five-year window before he has to truly face the world on his own.

"Man," Coach Jennings said after the lecture, "Coach Osborne made it so simple and clear why I got into coaching," Eric and James agreed. "I joined this fraternity because I wanted to impact the lives of young men the way that Coach Tom Nolen influenced me in high school," said Coach Jennings.

It was getting late. Coach Jennings told Eric and James to go get freshened up because they were going out with him that night. The two friends left, excited because they were going to hang out with a real big-time coach. It slipped their minds that Coach Jennings wasn't much older than they were.

Around six o'clock, Coach Jennings, Eric, and James met up to get supper. Jennings told them that the other coaches would be joining them. Coach McClain of Cumberland State; Coach Jackson and Coach Mays of Florida Tech; and Coaches Donald Mason and Terry Martin of University of Avon in Georgia; all joined them. They were all big-time coordinators that James and Eric were pumped about meeting. Quietly, James was wondering why a coach for a rival school was spending so much time with Eric and himself, two nobodies. Coach Jennings took a sip from a flask kept in his blazer pocket.

Eric and James, whom Coach Jennings began to refer to as "E & J"—pun intended—soon found out that these coaches were really "off the chain" with down-to-earth personalities. The group ate at Hooters in downtown Chicago.

After the restaurant, they ended up at a strip club called Maidens, and all Eric and James could think of was the Mickens Club story from earlier. Nevertheless, they tagged along with the group of coaches, some of whom made six-figure salaries and were on university travel per diems. Coach Jackson and Coach Mays from Florida Tech had just finished coaching in a New Year's Day Bowl game and had earned a $50,000 bonus!

Shortly after they arrived at Maidens, Coach Martin asked the waitress to send over five strippers, and tipped the waitress $100. Coach McClain was cozying up to one of the strippers, whom he told that "coaches and strippers go together like cookies and cream!" He wasn't joking! When the strippers found out there were coaches in the house, their performances went into overdrive. James was startled when a foghorn sounded and the lights began to flash and flicker—green, then yellow, finally red and then repeated. It seemed like there were strippers coming out of the damn floor. Leaning over to Eric, James said, "Dollars drop, asses POP!" Eric didn't remember that part of the Mickens story.

Eric looked around but he could not find Coach Jennings anywhere. "There he is!" James exclaimed, pointing but focused on the exquisite lap dance being administered by Sapphire—a name so cliché, but so appropriate. The pasties on her nipples twinkled in the club light. James was sipping Bud Light, thinking about getting right.

"In the corner, over there!" Eric looked over just as Jennings disappeared under a table and between a stripper's legs to commit, in public, a sexual act that should be reserved for adult films! But that wasn't enough. The stripper pulled him from under the table. Once he resurfaced, she positioned herself on the table, contracted her legs to reveal her eggs, and Coach Jennings dove in again. Just then James and Eric saw cigarette lighters flicker and phone cameras came out. Oh shit!

"I would've guessed the stripper would be giving him a blowjob," James said, "but damn, it's Coach Jennings under the table first and now atop the table, and that stripper is loving it!"

It was a little noisy in the place and it sounded like she kept saying, "1st and 10!" over and over. Come to find out she had a lisp and was actually saying, "You're the man!" The question became when he could come up for air. Like a bear from hibernation, Coach Jennings rose wiping his face, but no one said a word. They all just kept drinking and partying. The music kept bumping, the girls kept dancing, and the coaches kept spending.

Maidens had never seen anything like this group of coaches before. It was a tiny club off the beaten path that didn't get much action. Eric and James tried to be cool and calm, but the more they drank, the worse they became. They ended in the VIP room with three strippers and didn't leave until 4:00 a.m.

On the way back to the hotel, Coach Jennings told Eric and James that the staff was meeting with Coach Charley at 8:00 a.m. He had forgotten to tell them earlier. They were upset with Jennings for not mentioning this earlier, but it was too late for that battle. The coaches made it back to the hotel at 5:00 a.m. They ended up in the hotel restaurant drinking coffee and eating breakfast because they knew if they went to sleep, they might not make it to the eight o'clock meeting. Coach Jennings suggested that they go take a bath, but not go to sleep.

At the early morning meeting, it was obvious that the graduate assistants had been out all night, while Coach Jennings looked refreshed – not like someone who had just pulled an all-nighter. Eric and James could tell this was not his first time staying out all night. He had obviously done it many times before. Coach Charley advised everyone of the schedule for the upcoming recruiting weekend that would follow the convention. He wanted a status update on the recruits who were coming. The meeting lasted for one hour, but for the two grad assistants, it seemed like eight hours! After he concluded the meeting, Coach Charley said, "Let me talk to Eric and James." The two went into panic mode.

Eric wondered to himself how Coach found out. I knew he had spies! Eric thought. He was about to apologize for his actions the night before, but James cut in and said, "What's up, Coach?"

"I just wanted to know how your first convention's going so far," he said, "and I apologize for not being around to introduce some of my buddies. If you stay in this business, you'll find out what the old coaches do at the convention."

Eric and James gave each other a look that said, "You just don't know!"

"We met Coach Robinson on the elevator, and he said to tell you hello."

After they left the room, Eric said, "I hope his night wasn't like ours!" They finally got back to their room and passed out, and the next time they were seen was at O'Hare.

4 WIN

About a week or so after returning from the conference, James told Eric about a head coaching position opening up possibly for State University coaching staff member. Coach Charley had called Fred Davis into the office to inform him that Jamestown State University's Athlete Director was seeking permission to talk to Fred about their head coaching vacancy. Coach Davis had been a hot name in the coaching world for the last three years. His scheme was always popular with players and entertaining for fans. Under his tutelage, State U's offense ranked in the top ten in all major offensive categories for the last three years. Of all the hot coordinators in the country, Coach Davis was white hot. The only thing that could possibly keep him at State was either a fat raise or his teenage daughter complaining about changing high school during her junior year.

James had always told other coaches that Fred had a great offensive mind, which athletic directors and fans loved because offense put fans in the stands. Defense wins the games and championships, but who pays to see a perfectly executed weakside corner blitz from a cover two look? You don't know what that means. Who cares? You go to the games to see touchdowns—long runs and long passes. Coach Davis' offense delivered with the benefit of the Beast and yours truly, John Manning, star tailback. But, I digress. Since Coach Davis was so meticulous – clean shaven, dressed neatly, and spent a lot of time in front of the mirror – rumor had it that he was on the "down low." No one could confirm this rumor, but one thing was true – he was a damn good football coach.

Coach Charley cut right to the chase after alerting Fred of the situation. "Is it something you would be interested in?" Coach asked.

"You know it's been my dream to become a head coach," Fred replied.

"Well, Fred you know that I'll do all that I can to see that this happens for you."

Coach Charley had seen a lot of coaches come and go, but it was going to hurt to see Fred leave. He knew that he didn't have much more time in his career because he was getting older. As Fred left the old man's office, he knew that he had a lot to do to make this happen. He started making phone calls to head coaches and peers who would give him recommendations for the JSU job. In all, he had about six coaches call Dr. Calvin Jordan, Athletic Director at JSU, and still he wasn't sure if this was enough people to call. He knew it was going to fall on Coach Charley's recommendation. Despite his age and relative mediocre record over the past five years, the "what have you done for me lately" culture that pervades college football today still revered Coach Charley. Fred figured that he could still make a command call—say the word and perhaps get him the JSU job.

Fred researched and found out that Dr. Jordan and Coach Charley had started out coaching together over thirty years ago as graduate assistants, but Dr. Jordan went into administration, and Coach Charley became a coaching legend. Fred wanted the job, but now that the prospect of becoming a head coach lay before him, he was nervous and insecure. How could he be sure that he had done enough to merit the position? What in his past could disqualify him? In a panic, Fred wanted some assurance from Coach Charley that he had a real shot at the job. Meanwhile, to ensure his chance of becoming the man at JSU, Davis was going to pound on Coach to find out what kind of chance he really had at the job. At that thought, Fred received a call on his cell phone. "Hello?"

"Yes, is this Mister Frederick Davis?" On the other end was a very distinguished gentleman reminiscent of what a Rhodes Scholar might sound like. If they have a particular voice, but the fact is this person was highly educated. "Yes, this is Fred Davis. May I ask who's calling?"

"Yes, of course, Mr. Davis, this is Dr. Calvin Jordan, Athletic Director at Jamestown State University."

Fred almost pissed his pants! While he knew the call was coming, he couldn't have prepared himself for that moment. He tried to settle himself as Dr. Jordan started with the pitch.

"Fred, I don't want to pull any punches," Dr. Jordan started, "but I have been following your career for some time, and I think you are just the man to put JSU on the map. I'd like to fly to Baltimore tonight to speak with you further, and if all goes well we can start talking contract. Do you have any representation?"

"That's fine with me!" answered Fred before he heard the last part. "Representation? No, sir, I don't have any representation. Do I need some?" Dr. Jordan informed Fred that he would contact Coach Charley and get him set up with an agent. "Son, you're moving up in the ranks, step up and be ready."

After an interview with Dr. Jordan, Coach Davis accepted the job. He was then left with the task of putting together a staff. He went to the office intent on thanking Coach Charley; additionally, Fred wanted to talk to some of the coaches on State University staff about joining him at JSU. This was a common practice and would come as no surprise to Coach Charley. The natural progression of a coach was from assistant to coordinator to associate head coach to head coach. Head Coaches raid one another's staff routinely because it was about winning at all costs.

Fred didn't see Alice when he got to the office, so he knocked on Coach Charley's door. Coach welcomed him in and congratulated him again on his milestone.

"Coach, I've been working on putting together my staff," Fred said. "I'm offering Eric Person, your tight end coach my assistant head coach and offensive line position. I've also selected Tad Moore, the linebacker coach, as my defensive coordinator; Thames Keys, the wide receiver coach, as my offensive coordinator; and your offensive grad assistant, James Ryan Leaf, as my running backs coach."

"Damn son, you want my youngest son and my dog, too?" They both chuckled. Coach Charley asked, "What about Eric Fellows?"

"Well," Fred replied, "I would love to bring Eric on board, but my staff is complete, and I have some other coaches coming with me that I have known and worked with in the past."

"Oh, ok. I understand."

James and Eric had spent two years as GAs and they now needed to find jobs. Coach Davis's timing was perfect. Eric had been so excited about the chance to join Coach Davis's staff that he'd been discussing the possibility with his parents and friends. During their last conversation, Coach Davis had not given him a definite answer, but Eric told his girlfriend Angela that he felt good about his chances. A few days later, Eric asked James what was up with Coach Davis's staff picks.

"It's has been a week and he hasn't contacted me about the job at JSU," Eric said.

Eric was so hopeful and faithful, that he and Angela frequently prayed during this time. Eric began proclaiming his position inwardly and outwardly presuming that he had a position on Coach Davis' staff. Consequently, he asked if James had heard anything about when they should report to Jamestown. "Hell, Coach Davis has to hire us first, right?"

James had been avoiding this for quite some time. He knew Coach Davis wasn't going to hire Eric, but he felt so bad that he had just been avoiding Eric like a plague. "Um, I don't know what the job status is," James lied, but added that he was leaving the next day to start recruiting in Houston since Coach Davis had sent him money, a credit card and business cards by Federal Express.

Eric had a strange look on his face when James finished telling him about the recruiting trip. "He didn't tell you when I should report?"

"You gotta take that up with Coach Davis, man," James said, dropping his head, "You know I've got a lot of things to do before I fly out to Houston."

Eric left James and went straight to Coach Charley's office. He knew the old man could find out from Coach Davis what was going on with the job. He arrived at the office. Coach Charley came to the door and asked Eric to come in, saying that he'd been meaning to contact him. Eric walked in and immediately asked if he'd heard from Coach Davis.

"Calm down," Coach Charley began. "Yes, I met with Coach Davis before he left town. And no, he's not going to hire you."

"That's bullshit!" Eric exclaimed. He couldn't believe his ears. "Straight bullshit! I work my butt off every day! I gave him 100% as a player, he saw me give 100% percent as a coach, and he won't hire me. That's fucked up! That's not right!" Closing the door to his office

"It was a numbers game," Coach said. He tried to make Eric understand that Coach Davis only had room for one young coach, and he had chosen James.

"But, why?"

"You'll understand if you stay in this business, that as a coach you form relationships with many people. And as you form these relationships, you make promises." Coach Charley paused. "Coach Davis has a lot of friends, but you know he can't hire them all."

"Coach, all that may be true, but since I have been here, no one has ever outworked me. He knows I'm a better coach than James. I see now that Coach Davis is still screwing me. He screwed me as a player, and he's screwing me as a coach." With that, he stormed out the office while Coach Charley was talking, "don't do something today that you'll regret later."

Alice had seen the familiar look on the face of Coach Charley in years past. She knew how much Coach Charley cared for his players and coaches, but he was especially protective and fearful for his young GA's just entering the profession. Although recent college graduates, many GA's were naïve to the real world. Many were like Eric, hard-workers, but highly idealistic about the way things should be, how the profession should operate; however, young coaches like Eric either washed-out and the first sign of rejection or used that rejection to fuel a decent career. At this point, Coach Charley had no idea, which path Eric was on.

When he returned to his apartment, Eric broke down crying. He had put so much into this opportunity that it had started to blind his reality. Angela tried to console him, but Eric wasn't having it. This was a major disappointment. During his time as a player and as a coach, all he had ever known was disappointment.

Eric's mind returned to the golden days when he was a First Team All-State running back, capping one of the most celebrated careers in state history in terms of carries, yards from scrimmage, and touchdowns. Despite this, he had only been recruited by small schools. He remembered every disappointing moment at State University, beginning with the broken right ankle he suffered as a redshirt. Next, there was a pulled groin muscle as a freshman, and so on.

Angela had prepared Eric's favorite meal, lobster, and crab linguine. She brought Eric a plate and a glass of Merlot in an attempt to soothe his pain. Eric appreciated her attempts to console the inconsolable. He gently kissed her extended hand, pulling her close. Angela rested in his lap and began to feed him his dinner as he talked between bites.

"What hurts the most, Baby, is that the decision was not based on merit." Angela nodded while continuing her futile efforts to both console Eric and get him to eat. He chewed on that first bite for what seemed like hours while he talked, mumbled, sobbed, and raged about his undoing at the hands of Coach Davis.

"Baby, as hard as I worked, I was never truly given an opportunity to contribute on that offense. I knew the scheme inside and out, the checks, the formation adjustments, everything. I mean, I'm no John Manning, but I wasn't chopped fucking liver. Each time, I crept my way up the depth chart, Coach Davis would invent some reason to hold me back; he would find some reason to place an overvalued Ju-Co transfer ahead of me; he would nitpick my technique and question my effort. Son of ..." Angie cut Eric off with a large piece of crabmeat, butter dripping onto Eric's chin and some resting on her cleavage. Eric noticed. Angie smiled. He led her to the floor and relieved much of his stress right then and there.

After a week passed, with constant prompting and encouragement from Angie, Eric returned to form. He was more resolute to become the best coach in the country—that was his stated goal as found on the refrigerator written in alphabet magnets.

Eric was summoned one day by Coach Charley to meet for lunch. Recruiting was officially over, but Eric continued trying his best to impress the coaching staff at State because he wanted to be hired as a full-time coach. He had been really upbeat about the possibility of becoming the new wide receiver coach and assumed this lunch was the old man's way of offering him a job.

At lunch, Coach Charley told Eric, "I've been really impressed by the way you bounced back from a small setback." He assured Eric that this was par for the course and that better times were ahead. Eric started to smile since he was expecting the good news. Coach went on to ask, "Do you feel like you're ready to take on a full-time coaching job?"

"Oh, yes," Eric replied. "I have been dreaming about this day!"

"Good. I have one of my former players looking for a coach, and I wanted to know if you were interested."

"Of course, I'm interested!" His mind was working overtime since he didn't know any former Bison who were head coaches.

"There won't be any need to interview; if you want the job, all you need to do is tell Coach Steven Adams."

"What school?" Eric demanded. "How big a school is it? Who's Coach Adams?"

"Sooner College," Coach Charley replied. "The Bucks. It's a small NAIA school in Oklahoma. I believe there are about a thousand students."

Eric was stunned. He was actually thinking that Coach Davis had gotten to the old man. Eric audibly mumbled, "You gotta be fucking kidding me?"

"What's that son?" Coach Charley asked.

"Coach, I'll let you know before the end of the week." It was becoming a regular occurrence for Eric to come home disappointed. He started to doubt the decision he had made about becoming a coach.

The phone rang. "What's up, Big E?" James asked on the other end.

Eric perked up and tried to sound happier than he really was. "Hey, man! Everything is going well."

"Good! I only have a minute. I'm about to board my flight to Los Angeles, and I was just calling to see how everything was going, and to ask you to tell everyone hello for me." After hanging up the phone, Eric felt very low and saw himself as a failure compared to his friend.

Friday rolled around and it was time for Eric to make his decision regarding Sooner College. Jobs were drying up quickly, and for most coaches, there was not a lot of movement happening. The job market was sparse for a graduate assistant with no experience. Eric made it over to Coach Charley's office. He said his hellos to Alice, and she told him that Coach was expecting him.

"Eric, have you made a decision?" the old man asked.

"I have," Eric replied, "but I have one question for you, Coach. Why didn't you hire me since you have three job openings?"

"That's a fair question," Coach Charley started. "Eric, you're just not ready for the demands that I'd put on you here. It may be okay for other coaches to hire young, inexperienced coaches, but I've been working too long. It's like I told you before – this is the path most coaches travel. Some get lucky, some don't. So Eric, what's your answer?"

Eric said he wanted the job, and the old man called Coach Adams. "Eric Fellows is your next coach."

"What position will I be coaching?" Eric asked. Coach Charley told Eric that he was the new defensive coordinator for the Bucks of Sooner College. Eric walked out of the old man's office feeling a lot better than when he came in because he had never imagined becoming a defensive coordinator.

Both Eric and James were now on a path that many have chosen, but few have completed, it was to them winning at all cost.

5 CELEBRATE

For James, the past few days had been a whirlwind. One day he awoke as a GA at State University but went to sleep as the Runningback Coach for JSU. Within hours, he was on a plane crisscrossing the region trying to secure verbal commitments for JSU and Coach Davis. James had to leave State University immediately. He was not prepared for the sudden change—a term used in football to describe the unexpected, but usually meant that there was either a turnover or special teams touchdown. For James, this was a life sudden change; therefore, he had to adapt quickly and board a plane to begin recruiting high school football players.

James was on such an emotional high that he didn't have time to count his blessings for this kind of opportunity. Unlike Eric, James certainly didn't have anyone to share this watershed moment in his life. This was part of James' own doing based upon his response to what had happened to his father.

For Eric, it had been the ultimate culture shock. He'd grown up in a diverse, middle-class area in Richmond, Virginia, so going to Sooner College took him out of his cultural comfort zone. Eric was now crossing the country headed for the heartland. Sooner College was the biggest thing going in the state. Sadly, many of the residents of the state of Oklahoma attach their physical wellness and self-esteem to the success of Bucks football. Bucks fans are indiscriminate front-runners in every sense. When the Bucks are winning, there are few fans louder; however, when the Bucks are losing, you can't find a Bucks fan with the Hubble Telescope, much less hear them. Eric was walking right into the culture of a state crazy about football because there isn't anything else going. Eric would sign a four-year contract. The Bucks signed a promising class of players, but at the time, it was very plausible that neither Eric nor the rest of the coaching staff would be around to coach these incoming freshmen as seniors. Eric reflected upon his arrival on campus of something Coach Charley told him. "This is part of the coaching journey."

Recruiting was finally over for James and the staff at JSU started preparing for spring practice. It was going to be very important because all the terminology would be new to the players. Even though James was familiar with the playbook, he would have to work extra hard to develop a style of teaching. How would he relate the information and schemes in the playbook to his players? James hadn't been a full-time runningback since middle school. What did he know about being a runningback?

As preparation, James collected a vast amount of books and videotapes to help his coaching transition. If you ask me, this was money spent for nothing. What was he going to glean from a videotape other than how to copy someone else's style? Like most young coaches, he had a hard time accepting help. Like any young "boss", as runningbacks coach, James had his "crew" and wanted to train them as he saw fit.

By the morning of the first day of camp, James had been studying his materials furiously. James was totally out of his element and in over his head. He was never one to study football because it always came easy to him. James' greatest fear was to have his players "sniff" out that he didn't have a clue when it came to coaching runningbacks. James always knew when his coaches were full of shit. He knew that his players would realize the same about him if he didn't get his shit together and fast.

James made it to the office around 7:00 a.m., an hour before the offensive meeting started. He felt that after watching his drills and technique tapes, he could sound knowledgeable during the meeting. However, before the meeting commenced, James wanted to hear a familiar voice, so he called Eric. In the past, Eric would've answered his cell phone in a panic, thinking that something was wrong. This time, he just yelled, "Hello?" into the phone, sounding disoriented and annoyed.

"What's up, man?" said James.

"Is everything alright?"

"Everything's fine," James replied, "I just wanted to see what was up with you."

Eric started to get agitated since it was 5:00 a.m. in Oklahoma. "Do you need anything, man? I'm still in bed."

"I just wanted to talk to my man before we start our meeting here, but since you're not up, call me later. We'll be out of meetings at eleven my time." Eric slammed the phone down and fell back to sleep as Angie stirred around the bedroom and made her way to the shower.

Over time, these early morning calls worked for both Eric and James. It was a good way for them to find a "center" to their lives. The calls kept them in contact, as they quietly tracked one another's careers. This was especially true for Eric since he believed that James got his job. Eventually, each call from James added more motivation to Eric's drive to become the best coach in the country and to one day, if their teams ever crossed paths, to kick James' ass. Understand that these two men are genuinely great friends, but uber-competitive to the extent that its "Katie bar the door" when the whistle blows. Eric was determined to show everyone, including James, that he was a good coach. I believe that if beating James, Coach Charley, and Coach Davis counted on it, that Eric would chop-block his own mother. That boy's got a problem.

Some of this drive and anger inside Eric can be traced back to his father. Not much is known about Eric's background, but Eric is actually a hybrid, a half-breed, a mulatto, or any other term used for a racially mixed child. Not even Angela knew this. When asked about his parents, Eric would never mention his father. He would praise his mother for raising him alone. In actuality, Eric was raised by two parents—his mother, a buxom blonde from Davenport, Iowa, and his father a handsome intellectual from Monrovia,

Liberia. To characterize the marriage relationship of Eric's parents as tumultuous would do a disservice to tumultuous relationships.

Eric's full name is Eric Drew Fellows Curran. Eric decided to drop his father's last name just before entering high school. He didn't want to be associated with the man in any way. Dr. Curran was an accomplished trauma surgeon that was well respected in the Richmond, Virginia community. The Curran Family gave the outward appearance of a wholesome American family – diverse, loving, and harmonious; however, behind closed doors, The Curran Family was anything but happy.

Dr. Curran was a functioning alcoholic that was verbally and physically abusive to Eric's mother and his older brother Jameson. Perhaps Dr. Curran thought young Eric was too young to beat on like a prize-fighter, but Eric watched enough beatings to know that he loathed his father. He vowed that his household would bear no resemblance to that of his childhood. Both Jameson and Eric overcame this upbringing to do some great things. For Jameson, well he went on to some really big things which we will get into later.

It was during one of these early morning calls that James would make a revelation that shocked Eric. Eric and Angela had always planned to start a family. Eric wondered where James stood on having a wife and children. "I will never trust a woman enough to make her my wife," said James. With a little prompting from Eric, James would go on to reveal the genesis of his disdain for women.

James had watched a woman destroy two men. There was a reason that James was not a highly recruited nationally despite the fact that his talent warranted such attention. The Beast had the grades, the on-field prowess, and other intangibles to be a big-time college quarterback. He never got the chance due to Alicia McWilliams—his father's longtime girlfriend. Alicia and "Dude" as James' father was known, became an item during James' freshman year in high school. Alicia was a full twelve years younger than Dude, just eight years older than James himself.

Alicia always seemed to have some sort of control over Dude in James' eyes. By his sophomore year, James was back living with his Mother—he had always blamed Alicia for orchestrating the entire situation. Dude eventually bought James a Chevy Blazer the summer before his senior year. James made a point to get around town and see all that he could—in terms of girls. James skipped the last two hours of classes to go get a little bit of quality time with Kimberly Glory. While on the Loop, James saw what he was sure was Dude's Silverado. He knew that it was Dude's truck when he saw Alicia in the passenger side fixing her hair. Pulling alongside them, prepared to give the familiar "double-honk and head-nod", James was stunned to find that the driver of the truck was NOT Dude, but literally, some other "dude." Alicia looked over and having seen James, her face turned cold and distant. James was crushed.

Eric wanted to know more about this but James wasn't able to talk about it further. After the early calls from James, Eric would always contemplate his future. On one occasion, he called to Angela—who was in San Diego trying to make a sale—after talking to James. He never called her that early as a rule when she was on the road. They had been living together since college. Thinking that Eric may be relocating someday, the semester after they became serious, Angie began taking full class loads, including the summer and CLEP'd out of as many classes as allowed. Although two years Eric's junior, Angela would graduate from State University one year after Eric. This was a remarkable testament to what people will do for love.

Once Eric landed the Sooner College job, he had considered asking Angela to marry him. He had been thinking of it for a long time but had not popped the question. He thought living in rural Oklahoma with a population of only a thousand people could make for some lonely and depressing nights, and

Angela was definitely the one for him. Truth be told, Eric was whipped. He needed some in-house, some of that "fo-sho" as we say down in H-Town. Angie was down, hell, she couldn't wait to jump that broom. The two of them had been dating since she was a freshman. She took a sales job and started her own consulting company to allow her to travel with him as his coaching career started to blossom. How can a man not fall in love with a woman that's willing to follow him to Jupiter and back?

During this one particular call, Eric was sort of silent and Angie tried to get the conversation going.

"Baby, you're not sounding right? What's happened down there? Whatever it is, you must know that we will get through it," said Angela. She had truly perfected the art of picking up the pieces for her man as he put his heart and soul into this coaching thing.

As he started to speak the words, his voice trembled and crack, "W-W-Will you m-m-marry meeee?"

Angela was caught so off guard, she replied, "Say what?!"

Now more resolute and confident, Eric stated clearly, "Angela, will you marry me?"

"Um, I can't do that," Angela replied. She had always been a practical joker. "I was going to break up with you because I can't date someone from Oklahoma. And I won't live there for damn sure."

"You're kidding, right?" Eric asked, stunned.

Angela giggled. "You know I am! But, are you sure you want to get married? We never discussed marriage before! Besides, I'm doing well with the consulting, but AGI-Enroad Media Sales is moving its corporate offices to Washington, DC. That's $62,000 per, baby."

"Well, would you think about it? You're all I think about, baby. I love you. I know that that's some real money fresh out of school, but I'm trying to build something and I need you with me. I can't do it without you."

Needless to say, Angela said yes. The couple got married two weeks before fall camp started at Sooner – his very first fall camp as a coach. It was a small, lovely ceremony that took place in Angela's hometown of Trenton, New Jersey. James came down to be part of Eric's special day. The two friends were glad to see each other, but things were different between them. One would have assumed, for example, that James would have been Eric's best man, but Eric gave that honor to a high school friend he hadn't seen in over three years. A false rumor started to circulate that James made the trip to Trenton for Angela and that there was a little hanky-panky going on between them. This is what people assumed caused the distance between the two friends-- not their jealousy and envy as far as career nor the arrogance and competitiveness about coaching. People truly believed that there was something between Angie and James.

To flash forward just a bit, Angela didn't really do much to dispel the notion of her and James having a thing. There were times when Eric could be "hell on wheels" at home. Despite his interpersonal struggles with communication and his relationship with Angela, he was his father's son. This meant that he could be a real son-of-a-bitch. He would drink a little bit; however, his primary problem was simply engulfing himself with football. He would not pay much attention to Angela. His abuse of Angela was more emotional and mental than physical.

Angela knew just how to play Eric—ignore him. She would turn to James for emotional comfort. It was really nothing more than talking. Angela would pour her soul out about how Eric was treating her; but, James would simply say, "Everything is going to work itself out. You two will be okay." They would hug. Occasionally, James would workout a cramp in Angela's neck. Who knows? There were times that had James made a move, he could have had Angela again. At least that's what everyone thought. Eric seemed totally oblivious and everyone left him in the dark. More than anything, Eric wanted not only to start a family, but he wanted to keep his family together—for better or for worse.

The night before Eric's bachelor party, James was walking through the mall and crossed paths with Angie. At her suggestion, they stopped at Friday's for a drink and a chat.

"You know, I never thanked you for your maturity, discretion, and most of all for your silence," said Angela. A smiling James could only nod as he allowed Angela to continue. "I realize that I met Eric months later, but typically, men can't hold that type of information in." In response, James offered a simple comment and then opened up to Angela in stunning fashion. "Listen, when Eric brought you to the dorm that day to introduce you, it was clear that his nose was open. That's my boy. Who am I to ruin his parade like 100% rain?" Continuing, James said, "I can keep a secret like NSA. My Dad's girlfriend used to cheat on him. She even had other guys driving his truck; screwing them in his bed; spending his money on them; nevertheless, he loved her."

As you would expect, Angela wanted to know more: Why didn't James say anything? Did Dude ever suspect anything? James simply continued with regards to specifically addressing Angela's queries.

"My dad was a good man to that bitch. I caught her messing around on him. But this is how cold of a woman she is right here: I never forgave her for getting my dad to kick me off to my mom's house. I didn't say anything immediately because she took the first opportunity to offer some bullshit explanation. In response, I told her that she had two days to tell my Dad what was going on."

James paused. Angela could see that tears were beginning to well up in his eyes. Would this be the breakthrough moment? "James, you know that you can talk to me. Tell me what's wrong," begged Angela. "She didn't tell him. A couple weeks go by. My dad is falling harder and harder for her. I didn't want to be the one to break his heart. He loved Alicia. She's eating it up. He called me into his study one evening and showed me a ring. I couldn't take it anymore. I went to her job and told her that if she didn't call my dad right then and tell him that she was cheating, that I would tell when he got home. She didn't call. I went back to school and was going to tell him after practice, but I never got the chance."

Before practice that day, James was called into the Coaches Offices. When he walked in, there sat Dude, Alicia, Coach Barnes, and the Campus Substance Abuse Monitor (SAM). According to the SAM, operating on an anonymous tip, an ounce of weed was found under the driver's side seat of James' Nissan 300Z. There were several "doobies" in the ashtray. Coach Barnes convinced the SAM not to report the incident based upon James' potential college career and the personal pledge to bench James for the district championship game. James couldn't out Alicia to Dude now; although, he was sure that she was behind this setup. If he did tell Dude about her it would look like he was shifting blame or trying to divert attention from his own mistakes. Dude was big on accepting responsibility. James didn't smoke weed and everybody knew that he didn't. But the disaster didn't stop there. Somehow Southwest Mississippi, Florida, Virginia Tech, and Georgia got wind of this weed episode. James was immediately removed from their recruiting boards. It was a rap for big-time college football for James.

"Did you ever tell your Dad?" asked Angela.

"It hurt him because I waited until the wedding ceremony. But I had to hurt that bitch. Let her think that she was getting away with it. I was my dad's best man. The pastor asked for the rings and I let the bitch have it front of everybody. It was the only way to do it. My Dad is thankful but still hurt. We didn't speak for a while, until just before he passed. I got screwed out of a great college program experience and my dad died with a broken heart. I ain't got shit for women."

James is sobbing uncontrollably at this point. Angela tries to console him while also moved to tears. She gets him to his feet and they make it to a restroom. As he enters, James turns back to Angela with hand extended. She grasped his hand and entered the Men's Restroom with James. Inside a stainless steel stall in that mall, James took Angela from the back and worked out his anguish, grief over the loss of his father, and his hatred for women like Alicia. Angela could barely walk out of the restroom afterward. They would sit on a kiosk bench and talk for two more hours as she recovered. James and Angela's hooking up was a surprise to both of them despite their history.

Interestingly, Eric faced a similar situation with his own father. When Eric was twelve years old, he walked in on his father receiving fellatio from a dental assistant from a local office. Eric's class went on a field trip that day that was canceled due to rain. Eric's Mom was at work and had arranged for a neighbor to pickup Eric from school. Having arrived home two hours early, all parties involved were surprised. Eric was not supposed to be home. His father was not supposed to be home. The young concubine milking Dr. Curran for all he was worth did not live at the house. Eric never told his Mom. He knew that she would confront Dr. Curran and suffer a beating for the insurrection. However, Eric's disdain for his father continued to grow.

What took place previously between Angie and James was that Angie came to State University for a tour during the second semester of her Senior Year at North Trenton High. James was part of the welcoming committee that would provide the prospective students with some insight into the ambiance of State. He and Angela didn't immediately connect, but she was reassigned to his tour group just before lunch. During lunch, held in the massive State U. Student Activity Center, James began to catch Angela's eye a bit. James sensing the curiosity of the hot little would-be coed began to turn on the charm. Mix in a little attraction with the curiosity, the only thing left was opportunity, which came when the tour group made it to the dormitories. James called ahead to Sorority Row alerting them that he had some prospective pledges in his group. That move took care of seven young ladies for an hour. As for the four fellas, he told them where they could find the women's track team practice. Boom they were out of the way, which left, student #12, according to her visitor's badge—Angela. She would accompany James to Session Hall. They would swing an episode for about fifty-three minutes. They would be able to cleanup swiftly and make it back to the Student Center within the hour James had allotted.

"Eric believes that he got it, but you know that I gave you my virginity, right?"

"I am aware of that and I always appreciated being your first. But remember, Eric is your last and your everything," James stated with emphasis.

"You mean, you never contemplated what we could have been?" asked Angela bluntly.

"No. Never. Not once. It was a good time. A cool release and for that to have been your first time, you'd obviously done some research. But no. The next time I saw you, you were with Eric. Done deal."

With that statement, the two rose from the table, embraced, James paid the tab, and they exited in opposite directions. They would see one another again at the wedding.

After James made it back to Virginia, he had personal decisions to make in his own life. He was young and had had a rocky start back at State University as a player, but now he struggled with being a Division I coach at age twenty-three. He didn't have a serious love life. He was dating a young lady he met at a club in Jamestown, but he was not serious about her. It was his relationship with Sherry, a JSU student that almost doomed his career. Sherry was a beautiful brunette, a work-study student for the athletic department. She was nineteen years old and living every minute to the fullest.

Coach JR, as James was called around the office, started off talking and flirting with Sherry around the office as they worked. Finally, one day, James asked Sherry if she had a man in her life.

"Yes," Sherry replied.

"Are y'all serious?"

"Yeah, we've been dating since I came to school here two years ago."

James let that be the end of the conversation. Sherry, however, started the conversations back up, saying she needed more in her life. If Coach JR was interested, she said, she would make time for him.

For the next two years, James had a fling with Sherry that lasted until she graduated. She never asked a lot of him, just a few "nuggets" here and there. She would come to his office to ask if he needed her to do any work, and he would invite her to engage in sexual activities. Always, after she gave him a blowjob, Sherry had to have some chicken nuggets from KFC. For a blowjob, James couldn't beat that price! Buying her some chicken nuggets with honey mustard was like getting a penalty after a touchdown—who gives a shit, right? A win is a win.

This relationship would have gotten the best of James, if not for an unlikely person – Ms. Evelyn Jackson, the football secretary. Evelyn's importance at the JSU offices was equivalent to Alice at Coach Charley— nothing went on in the program without Evelyn knowing something about it. Nevertheless, Evelyn put Coach JR back on track. She'd protected Coach JR for quite some time in his relations with Sherry. Her multi-level defense system consisted of making up excuses for James when he was up to no good—missing meetings with players, coaches, or late to practice.

Ms. Jackson thought a lot of him, so one day she pulled him to the side, and said, "Watch yourself, because you don't want to ruin your career on this seasonal girl. I know she's cute and got a little back, but she changes men like I change shoes! Just watch yourself, baby."

73

She ended the conversation by telling James, "Be safe. And please, for your sake, keep that young lady away from your office." The young coach took Ms. Jackson's advice to heart. He started handling himself better at the office, and not being so disrespectful to the program by flaunting his "jump-off" all around the coaches' offices.

At Sooner, Eric was finding out that he truly had to coach—he had to come up with game plans; and, he had to manage his side of the ball. Since he was a coordinator, it was much more complicated than the arguments he and James would have on the whiteboard as graduate assistants. These arguments usually consisted of discussing how one could devise a better scheme than the other. It would get very heated between them. They had yet to find out what the older coaches already knew – the game on the dry-erase board was always won by the last one with the marker in his hand.

Eric learned so much about coaching at Sooner. Coach Adams was a great guy to work for because he would always defer to Eric, giving him full rein of defense. Coach Adams was elated with his young charge and wanted him to enjoy his own learning curve. Adversity would shape this young coach early in the season as his schemes begin to be picked apart and he would rack his brain to make adjustments on the fly. Coach Adams wanted his coaches battle-tested, tried by fire if you will, early in their careers. It would be the response to this early misfortune on the field that would be most important for Eric. But let's be real, Coach Adams has no interest in a 0-5 start due to his defense. He had no problems stepping in if Eric was just stinking up the place. In any event, Eric would only have to inform him of the game plan when reporters asked questions so that he was able to answer them without sounding like an idiot.

Coach Adams was a young coach, around thirty-four. He had been a walk-on running back for State University and went on to become a successful high school coach in Texas. He won four state championships in seven years at Houston Lamar and was offered an opportunity to be the defensive coordinator at West Texas State. After a year, he became head coach at Sooner, a school that had fallen on hard times because of ineligible players and fighting. He was in his second season at Sooner, and things were moving in the right direction.

When Eric arrived at Sooner, he assumed there would be this huge coaching staff, but what he found was that only he and Coach Adams were full-time. The rest of the staff consisted of two student coaches trying to finish their undergrad degrees, four part-time coaches, two resident dorm counselors and two admission counselors. Eric would often act as if he was having a defensive staff meeting when James called – little did James know that Eric's defensive staff was a staff of one.

Both Eric and James seemed to be on the right path. Eric was cultivating his coaching abilities at Sooner, and James had started to really mature as a coach at Jamestown. Eric would go to Jamestown in the spring to clinic with the coaching staff there. Coach Davis had really opened doors for Eric to view films and discuss schemes. Coach Davis never knew the animosity that Eric held towards him; however, for Eric, the gesture of Coach Davis' allowing him access to the staff was invaluable and cathartic.

After two years at Sooner, Eric felt it was time to move on, and as fate would have it, Jamestown had a defensive end coaching position open. During one of his early morning conversations with James, he asked his friend to put in a word to Coach Davis about the open position. James said this wouldn't be a problem, and that he would help in any way that he could.

Eric called the old man, Coach Charley, asking him to contact Coach Davis as well. He hadn't talked to Coach Charley much since he left for Oklahoma. When he finally got through to the old man, his first words were, "Coach, I need your help."

"That's not a problem," Coach Charley replied.

"Could you call Coach Davis and act as one of my references for the defensive end position?"

"Yes, I will. I'll be glad to."

After two weeks, Eric hadn't heard from Coach Davis, even though he'd left several voice messages to him. It took an early morning ritual for Eric to receive an answer. "Is Coach Davis going to interview me?" he asked James during one of their phone calls.

"Coach has already hired some guy," James said, "and I just assumed that he'd gotten in touch with you to tell you."

Eric was distraught after hearing this. He hadn't felt this way in years — it was that familiar feeling of failure. He went home for lunch, where he and Angela discussed the news.

"You have to persevere," Angela told her husband. "I love you, and I will always support you."

"Do you see this shoe box?" Eric asked, pointing to a box full of papers on the kitchen table. "It's full of rejection letters, and I've been keeping that box ever since I was a grad assistant. It used to drive me to keep fighting, but now, it's starting to become a reminder of my constant failures." Angela had learned to let her husband's mood swings run their course. He always wore all his emotions on his sleeve.

"Look at each letter in that box as a brick in the house that you're building as a coach."

Eric sighed. "You can't build much as a $30,000-a-year coach. If they were paying me six figures like James, it'd be different." He paused for a moment. "You know, baby, James can't even hold my jock when it comes to coaching. All he knows how to do is what they tell him to do."

Angela sort of snapped. Maybe it was the realization of the money James was making; maybe it was her weariness of Eric's bitchy mood swings and constant need for consoling, but she snapped.

"You know what, to hell with this! To hell with you and your bruised ego and your feelings! I don't care about those letters! And I don't care how you feel about those letters anymore! I wipe my ass with those letters, what they represent to you, and how you feel about them!"

"Honey, you need to lower your tone and I mean, fast!"

"Don't you raise your voice at me! I am three months pregnant asshole and you need to get your shit together!"

The couple had suffered through two miscarriages. Angela was not carrying a viable fetus. Eric couldn't believe his ears. He rushed over to her for she was now sobbing uncontrollably. They were both crying. Angela was imploring Eric to provide for their child. Eric was promising to do what it took to earn more money in coaching. Their lives would never be the same.

Eric was convinced that neither Coach Charley nor James helped him get the position at JSU. He could only see the system fighting against him again. If he'd had any doubt before about Coach Davis having something against him, it was put to rest by this most recent rejection. It took Eric about a week not to be too busy to receive his early morning ritual call from James.

James had been holding back on telling Eric that he wasn't happy at JSU and that he'd truly become the "you do only what I say" coach on the staff. James was smart enough to know that he needed to get out while he still had a chance. He started looking on the Internet and in the newspaper to see what was happening in the coaching job market. He would check out the "J-Coach" website – a site that all coaches would go to for the latest gossip, rumors, and of course, the new job postings – searching for any little scoop that he could find. James knew the good thing about being a Division I football coach was that people would return your call.

In his search, James found out there was an opening at Bankhead University in suburban Atlanta for a wide receivers coach. He remembered the coach that he met at his first convention, with whom he'd formed a relationship. He was very apprehensive to leave because of his loyalty to Coach Davis, but he knew he'd always be fond of JSU. James made calls to Coaches Donald Mason and Terry Martin from the University of Bankhead, and the next thing he knew he was flying to Atlanta to meet with the school's head coach, Coach Manavich.

James went by Coach Davis's house the night before his flight and asked Mrs. Davis if he could speak with her husband. Mrs. Davis let James in and told him that Fred was in the study. James was so nervous because this was his first job. "I got something to tell you," he stammered as he entered the study.

"James, relax," Coach Davis cut him off. "I spoke with Coach Manavich two days ago and told him you would make a great hire. I was just hoping you would come to me. It's good for you to take this opportunity." James was so surprised at what he was hearing. "Head coaches talk to each other," Coach Davis smiled, "and they normally inform each other about such moves, just as a courtesy. Unless a coach doesn't like you."

James felt that if he told Eric immediately, Eric would be disappointed with his new job, so he waited a while to tell his friend the news. When he got the opportunity to tell Eric about Bankhead, he made it seem like he was contacted by Coach Manavich, but Eric took the news in stride.

Things did change for Eric. He got a call from Central Tech University in Kansas about an opening on their staff. He had a meeting with Central Tech's head coach, Sherman Traylor, in the airport at the World Football Coaching Association Convention. The two struck up a conversation at the bar, and Coach Traylor wanted to know if Eric was interested in a move. "Yes," Eric said, "because I'm ready for a step up in talent." He knew that he would become a position coach, but at least he would be coaching in Division I-AA, and he felt this was the next step to big-time coaching.

What he didn't know was that Central Tech was at the bottom of the barrel in football. They hadn't been competitive in years, and they had a reputation as a coaching graveyard. Central Tech had only won 20 games in the last 10 years. This was an average of two wins per year; only Columbia University and Prairie View A&M University had ever had a longer span of futility. But no one could tell Eric anything. He felt that if he could somehow turn Central Tech around, then the sky was the limit. Eric was happy to get another job because this was a step-up opportunity to show the world that he was a real coach. Now he had to explain the move to Angela that he had accepted a job without consulting her. He'd made one promise to her – that they would visit the next place before they made a decision to take a new job.

"Honey, I've got something to tell you," Eric said as he entered the apartment. Angela knew this wasn't a good sign.

"What's up?" she asked.

"I got an offer for a job at a bigger school!" To his surprise, Angela was excited. She knew that a bigger school had to mean a bigger city or town.

"Where is this job?" she asked. "When do we go visit?"

Eric got a funny look on his face and said, "Well, there is no visit to campus. I told Coach Traylor that I'd take the job."

Disappointed, she asked, "Where's the job located, and how much will you be making?"

"The job is in Kansas, and I don't know what he's going to pay me."

"Kansas??" Angela shouted. "What part of Kansas? Oz?? And why in the world would you take a job without knowing what you're going to make?"

"But, baby, we have to make this move! It's the next level!"

Eric went over to talk with Coach Adams and informed him that he got an opportunity to coach in Division I-AA. He told Coach Adams that he had enjoyed his time at Sooner. Coach Adams congratulated him and said that if Eric needed anything he should let him know. While Eric was talking with Coach Adams, Angela was on the Internet researching Central Tech University. She found out that it was in Topeka, population 20,000, and that the football program was one of the worst in the country. Angela was not very happy, but she supported her husband.

The thought of living in such a small environment was starting to close in on Angela. She knew people in the Midwest who couldn't find jobs in their degree field. Eric and his soon-to-pop wife made it to Topeka. They were dealing with a lot of drama in their lives – a new job, a new town, and a baby due any day. James, on the other hand, got the job at Bankhead and felt he could start fresh with a new staff and develop more friends.

Both James and Eric were about to start the next phase in the business of coaching.

6 FAVOR

The NCAA president acknowledged that intercollegiate athletics has an unflattering record of hiring women and people of color for leadership positions — particularly athletics directors and head coaches of high-profile sports. Since integration, there's been a debate in major college athletics about the number of coaches that should be on a football staff. There were questions about the roles of the respective coaches on the staff and the power hierarchy. This debate has crossed color barriers as more and more black men have entered the coaching profession. Furthermore, as intercollegiate athletics in general and football, in particular, began to garner huge fees for broadcasting rights and break records in terms of merchandising, politics entered the equation. Head coaches were commanding seven-figure salaries. Now more than ever, voices decrying the lack of black head coaches in college football were growing.

Since Johnny Cochran and his partners came to prominence, the Black Coaches Association has fought for acceptance, and the battle lines have been drawn. There are but 14 minority head coaches among all football-playing member institutions (excluding historically black colleges and universities). Most conservative estimates indicate that at the apex of employment the number of black head coaches represented 2.4 percent of all head football coaches. This was a pitiful statistic given that 55 percent of all student-athletes playing football are African-American. Still today, can you believe the racist attitude of our society reflected in the number of minority head coaches?

In the past few years, there had been only a nominal increase in the number of black head coaches in the Football Bowl Subdivision (formerly Division I-A). At that rate, it will take more than 80 years before the NCAA reaches a percentage that even approximates the number of African-Americans in the general population. Not only is the status quo unacceptable, it is unconscionably wrong. Everyone knows it—especially the University Presidents and Athletic Directors—they just don't have any real pressure to do anything about it.

Some people advocate a "Rooney Rule" for college football, who knows, I'm just a player, but I may want to become a coach someday after my NFL career is over. I would like to believe that I would have a legitimate shot at running a program one day rather than just contributing to its success. The Rooney Rule put in place in the NFL requires teams filling head coaching vacancies to include a person of color among their interviewed candidates. Teams that do not abide by that rule face a significant fine. Arguably, such a rule will not work for higher education, nor can a specific sport be singled out to operate apart from the institution. More importantly, the NCAA contends that such a rule is not necessary. Ostensibly with the help of the Black Coaches Association annual publication of a Hiring Report Card, about 30 percent of all final candidates interviewed over the past three years for Division I head coaching positions have been African-American.

Notably, 76 percent of all the openings have had at least one minority candidate interviewed. In effect, the report card and the resulting publicity attendant to it has been functionally equivalent to the Rooney Rule, let the NCAA tell it. There must be some pressure to force these Presidents and Athletic Directors to pull the trigger to hire qualified black head coaching candidates. Eric and James couldn't worry about the big picture and staff breakdowns. They could only see what they had to do for themselves—get a job and stay employed. Both knew that though they had jobs, racial discrimination—in the sense that the public outcry and media pressure to hire black coaches would only intensify. As a consequence, the push-back from the "good ole boy" network controlling the hiring decisions at the big-money state schools would be equally fierce. In the twinkling of an eye, it seems that race could alter their careers.

While others debated the race issues in the profession, Eric started to blossom into a decent coach. Coach Charley kept tabs on both James and Eric, as much as he could. Quietly Coach Charley confided in Alice that Eric was laying the foundation to become a great coach. His recruiting had improved, and Central Tech University ended up becoming a great move. The job at Central Tech University exposed Eric to a growing, racially diverse culture that included a majoring instance of interracial marriages. I won't go into some sort of anthropology lesson here, I play football and my girlfriends write papers on such things. Don't get me wrong, I did my work, but there were times that I just wasn't in the mood for articulating my thoughts in detail on four to five typewritten double-spaced pages.

After one season at Central Tech University, Eric applied for a position at Mississippi Tech in Jackson, the largest city in Mississippi. The environment at Mississippi Tech had changed over the years, but the school had a long history of segregation. Mississippi Tech played in what was considered the best conference in the country, so a job like this could really propel Eric as a coach to be recognized. Eric was confident about the opening because he was very familiar with the coaching staff at Mississippi Tech. He had befriended many of them after Mississippi Tech played in a New Year's Day Bowl, and he called head coach Billy Miller to see if they would clinic with his staff. Coach Miller opened his doors, allowing Eric to spend two weeks with his staff as they prepared for spring practice. After he found out that the school's running back coach had left to take a job in the NFL, he got on the phone. Eric left a detailed message about his interest in the running back job. Once Coach Miller was able to get in touch with him, he asked Eric to fax over his resume with references.

Eric was excited about the prospect of coaching in the Old South Conference. When he returned home from his interview with Coach Miller, he and Angela had a long talk about what this job could do for his career. Angela was extremely burned out from all this job bullshit; she wasn't sure that she could make it all work. This new move would mean that Eric would be out chasing a dream while she'd be home dealing with a newborn baby. In her journal, she would log entry after entry over years wondering what her life would have been like had she not met Eric—and made something work with James.

Meanwhile, Eric was so consumed by the idea of being the next "Bear" Bryant that he was about to forsake all others! I am not sure that anything short of Angela asking for a divorce could derail Eric's single-minded locomotive drive to become the best coach in the country. Still, despite her feelings, Angela said, "Everything sounds great! This is a great opportunity for you to work in Mississippi." What she was really thinking was that she couldn't see herself living in Mississippi. Since Oklahoma and Kansas had been bad enough, but Mississippi would be like living in a foreign country! She missed New Jersey and the east coast and could not fathom living in the deep south.

"It's not like you think," Eric told his wife, trying to reassure her. "You have the wrong image of Mississippi. Jackson is a town of about 250,000 people."

"Whoopty-doo!" Angela replied sarcastically. "A town of 250,000." She advised. Actually, Jackson is larger than Angie's hometown of Trenton, but Eric dare not say that. Eric knew to tread lightly, but his single-minded focus always controlled him. He was always getting all worked up about the next great job, and he hadn't even been offered a job yet.

"This is different," Eric insisted. "I know these coaches, and I've developed a great relationship with them. Coach Miller all but told me I was going to get this job. Why do you always have to be so negative? Can't you be happy for me getting this chance?"

As Angela walked out of the room, she told him, "I'm not going to keep doing this!"

Eric was looking forward to the World Football Coaches Association Convention that year because Coach Miller was going to do the formal interview for the running back position during the convention. It was going to be held in Miami, so he knew this would be a great place to celebrate. It would be the first convention to which he would take his wife. Angela's parents were going to keep their son Kevin, and Eric thought the break would be a great way to get their marriage back on track.

Nothing in his past could have prepared Eric for what would meet him in Miami. He'd taken Angela from the central Atlantic region of the country to the heartland and the Southwest. Neither of them had ever been to Florida, much less Miami. Entering Miami International was a culture shock of cosmic dimensions for the young couple. There were beautiful people of all shapes, sizes, nationalities, ethnicities, all speaking English intermittently with their native tongue. The pace was dizzying. The couple deplaned, got lost heading to baggage claim—thus two other couples, a coed, an elderly woman, and a lawyer were lost as well because they were following Eric and Angela. "I was following you because you looked like you knew where you were going. Que idiota!" exclaimed la cubana Viejo.

Miami was beautiful. It was a thirty-minute cab ride from the airport to the Hotel in South Beach. The ride was akin to a scene from Scarface. The crystal blue water, palm trees lining the freeway, the marina, the planes flying low in preparation for landing. One thing that scared the living skin off Angela was the impatience of the drivers. "This reminds me of driving in Texas, but with smaller lanes," remarked Angela to the multi-tasking Haitian cab driver who simply turned and smiled as he looked from his Microbiology Today textbook. Angela couldn't imagine a place so bright. "Why have we never come here before, Eric?" Like a pure tourist, Angela stuck her head out of the cab window to let that Miami breeze soothe her face and scalp.

"Woman, get your crazy butt back into this car,' said Eric. "We're here now and that's all that matters. One day, I'll buy you a house here," he continued, trying to be serious.

While Eric was out doing his coach thing, Angela was meeting coaches' wives and having a great time. It was the first time Angela was able to talk with someone who felt like she did, and this was such an eye-opening experience for her. She really bonded with Beth Davis, the wife of John Davis, who was the head coach at Western Ohio University – a mid-major school that played some very good Division I-A schools. Beth and Angela shared lots of woman-to-woman talks regarding the intricacies of being the wife of a coach.

On the second day of the convention, James and Eric got together and had a chance to talk. Eric told his friend about his interview at Mississippi Tech. James told Eric he was happy for him, but it was obvious that things would never be the same in their friendship. It was difficult for Eric to suppress his contempt for James' situation—not him personally. They were still friends, but Eric was jealous. James knew and tried to work around. They could both feel the distance between them. A conversation was needed to address this tension between them, but as many women find out early as young girls, men don't generally talk things out or get to the bottom of situations and all that Oprah and Dr. Phil shit. All we can say is something similar to "Damn! My partner's trippin'. He'll get over it." That's about it. But, Eric wouldn't get over it. He wanted to get even and that meant out besting everyone—coach, administrator, athletic director, or even university president—that ever doubted him.

That night, Eric met Coach Miller at his suite for the interview. It was a very informal interview since they had developed a relationship with each other. Coach Miller told Eric to take a seat on the couch and asked if he wanted something to drink.

"No, thanks, Billy," Eric replied.

"So, do you think you could live in Mississippi?" Coach Miller asked in a thick Mississippi accent.

"Oh yeah," Eric smiled. "I can fit in anywhere in the south. I'm so passionate about college football in the south because that's where I want to coach."

"That's fine, but Mississippi isn't like most states. They still don't take well to people who don't speak like them."

It started to become apparent to Eric that Coach Miller was only giving him reasons not to coach at Mississippi Tech. Still, Eric kept pushing him and letting him know that he would give everything as a coach – loyalty, trust, and commitment. "This is where I was meant to coach," he insisted. Meanwhile, Coach Miller loved Eric's enthusiasm, not fearing that he wasn't equipped for the job. Coach Miller felt certain that Eric was not prepared for the larger socio-economic culture of Mississippi and the tangential football sub-culture. Coach Miller envisions this culture feeding on Eric and his young family like a school of barracudas if the team started to lose and his position players were underperforming.

"I have no doubt you would make a great coach," Coach Miller said. "I've gotten to know you over the years. You're going to be a great coach; however, my program is not in the position to make such a bold move. In short, my administration won't let me hire you."

"What do you mean, Billy?" Eric asked, stunned. "I know you have a job opening. The AD won't let you fill the position? Why?"

"I have a team that is 70% black right now, and I only have one black coach on a staff of fifteen. If I hire you, I don't think I'd be able to win the recruiting wars against the Southeastern Athletic Conference schools to get great players." Moreover, the Black Coaches Association is taking a more proactive role in ensuring that qualified black candidates get interviews. They're running a sophisticated media campaign using current black coaches in the NFL, those coaching in BCS member schools, and they've recently begun to target university endowments through threatened legal action. It's rough out here on the administrative side of football.

Eric hardly knew what to say. "That's unfair! I'm totally qualified for this position, which is just not fair! That's discrimination—reverse discrimination. I can sue! I'm familiar with those law school cases from Michigan, California, and Texas! I've got precedent on my side!"

Coach Miller just sat and sipped his drink while Eric continued to rail against the "machine" that was capping his coaching career with a glass ceiling before his very eyes. "Nobody should be forced to hire anyone, Coach. You should be able to hire the best candidate."

"You're right," Billy agreed, "but it's out of my hands. I wanted to interview you because I really respect what you're trying to do in this profession. But think about it. I can deal with media pressure over my hires. What I cannot deal with is sitting in a living room in Tupelo and having a kid and his parents tell me that he's not coming to Tech because there aren't enough coaches that look like him."

"Oh, bullshit! Who makes a university choice based on the race of the Coach?"

"Roy Sixkiller—top rated quarterback in the State of Mississippi. He loves Mississippi, came to all our camps since he was in the 8th grade. He loved the campus, still has close friends on the squad. But we have no Native American presence on campus, on the staff, or none of that. Bless his heart, but he went to Oklahoma State. The rest is history. He was voted co-Newcomer of the year. Who knows what tips the scales for a kid, but it's that sort of volatility that is squeezing you out at Tech, son."

Eric tried to remain composed, but he didn't know what he was going to tell Angela. He didn't know how he could pick up the pieces and make some new coaching connections in Miami while there was still time. Most of all, how could he enjoy Miami with his wife now, after having the job that he depended on vanish into thin air?

Eric walked out feeling deflated. He wasn't a prejudiced person, but at that moment, he felt like all black people got the easy route to jobs with this Affirmative Action fucking bullshit. He'd heard of coaches losing out on jobs because of their race, but that had seemed like a myth. Now he was experiencing it for himself.

Eric was so down that he couldn't face Angela. He was too afraid that she might say, "I told you so!" and talk again about him getting his hopes too high. He ended up on Ocean Drive at Casablanca's, a sidewalk restaurant with a live band and a great bar. It was far enough from the hotel that Angela would need to exert some effort to find him. He was depressed but struck up a conversation with three gentlemen there. He asked the guys if they were coaches, and they said that they were. There were two white coaches and one black coach. They noticed that Eric appeared down. The older coach, Travis, asked if everything was all right, and said that he hoped Eric was not at the convention looking for a job.

"No, I just finished interviewing for a job," Eric replied.

The black coach, Malcolm, asked, "Did it go bad?"

"No, but I didn't get the job because I'm white."

"Join the club!" Malcolm said. "I've lost plenty of jobs because I'm not white."

"Where do you coach?"

89

"At Jackson A&T, a historically black university in Mississippi."

"Wow!" Eric exclaimed. "The job I was interviewing for was Mississippi Tech."

Travis chimed in and told Eric to hang in there. He said that Eric didn't lose the job because he was white, but because society demanded that coaches do a better job of servicing the young men they're coaching. Following that statement, Eric was reminded of what Coach Miller was trying to say to him earlier. "I'm older than you," Travis went on, "and I can remember when there were no black coaches, or maybe just one in a conference. Did you hear me? In an entire conference."

"Maybe all those things are true, but I lost this one because of my skin color. I don't mind losing the job, but just hire the best candidate!"

Malcolm looked at Eric and said, "You mean that no black coach is more qualified than you?"

"No, I'm just saying I was the most qualified candidate."

"How do you know you're the most qualified candidate?"

Eric thought a minute and replied, "Maybe you're right. I don't know." "Mmm. Hmm," said Malcolm as he ordered a second South Beach Margarita. Eric decided to let the issue go for the night so that he could connect with his new peers.

The coaches had a good time talking and drinking. When they finished, they exchanged phone numbers. Eric left feeling much better, and he had a better understanding of the decision that was made.

He made it back to his hotel room at 4:00 am, and Angela was up worrying since he'd promised her earlier that they were going to spend time together. Angela met him in the foyer of the suite, "Why did you turn off your phone, asshole!" Eric pushed past her and settled on the foot of the bed. Then he sighed and broke into tears. "Baby, they didn't hire me," he cried. "I just don't know what's wrong with me."

Rolling her eyes as if to say, 'not again," Angela exclaimed "That's their loss!" trying to soothe her husband. "You don't need them! Fuck 'em. Yeah, I said it."

"Do you want to know why I didn't get the job?"

Angela looked lovingly at Eric and said, "No. I just know I love you. Let's go to bed now."

The next morning, on the last day of the convention, Angela told Eric that they were going to dinner with Beth and John. "I don't know them," Eric said, "and besides, I want to spend this last day with you." He gave her a flirtatious look.

"Oh, please," Angela said, rolling her eyes and slapping her husband's hand.

The couples met up for lunch at a great Cuban restaurant in downtown Miami. Angela introduced Coach John Fitzgerald Davis – no kin to Coach Fred Davis at Jamestown – and his wife Beth to her husband.

"Angela didn't tell me that you were a coaching family," Eric said. "I just assumed she'd met a local couple."

John replied, "I don't act like most coaches at the convention. This is my time to get away from that life." After a great lunch, John asked Eric, "What are you looking for in this business?"

"I thought I'd found it," Eric replied. "I interviewed for a position at Mississippi Tech, but I didn't get it." Eric didn't mention the race issue since John was black. He was unaware that John was a head coach at a Division I-A school. Since there were only four black coaches amongst the 120 Division I schools, maybe the name should have rung a bell.

"What position do you coach?" John asked.

"I've coached defense mainly, but I played offense at State University."

"You played for Coach Charley?"

"I played for him and was a graduate assistant for him."

"Coach Charley is one of my best friends," John smiled. "We were on the Head Coaches Council together."

Eric perked up a bit. Angela began to smile while staring into her plate. Beth was doing the same. The dinner and conversation were great. The two couples talked about family, religion, and life in general. Coach Davis asked, "How do you balance family with work?"

"You know, it's hard, but it's a direct reflection of my head coach. I've been blessed to work with coaches who don't grind. They stress that everyone should get in, get their work done, and then go home to spend time with their families." John really liked the answer. He told Eric that he had a position open for a wide receiver coach, asked if Eric would be interested.

"Sure! But where do you coach?"

"I'm the head coach at Western Ohio University," John said. "Let me get back to the office and have reservations made to fly you and your wife to Cincinnati."

Angela was so happy for her husband. The two had no idea that a wife could land a coaching job for her husband! Beth Davis was the one who initiated the contact. She had watched Angela bop around the hotel and invited her for coffee to chat. This was the second morning of the trip. As it turns out, from an anthropological standpoint, this situation was akin to a religious conversion. Coach Davis screened potential clients with the help of his wife. Just as religious missionaries seek out women in the countryside to convert first. Get the woman and you'll usually get an opportunity to the man.

Eric and Angela made it up to Cincinnati and accepted the job. Eric couldn't wait to call James. It was as if all the bad feelings toward him were gone since he now was a Division I football coach. James was happy for Eric, but he thought to himself, about his friend, "Eric, be careful what you wish for."

7 RECRUITING

To Angela's surprise, Eric made an amazing transformation after getting the job at Western Ohio. She would never have imagined that a job at a Division I school would make her husband more attentive and caring, but it did. Eric would come home from work, ask her about her day, and take time with their son, help with the dishes, and oftentimes fall asleep with his head in Angela's lap as she read Michael Eric Dyson, imagine that.

It also seemed like his relationship with James became better. He initiated more calls to James now, whereas before, James was the only one holding on to their friendship. Angela was proud of Eric; the new man he'd become reminded her of better times when the two former roommates would talk about football and coaching for hours as both pledged their loyalty to each other. Eric had it "going on" again and Angela thought that he "wore it" well. She remembered Eric telling her that in order to make it in coaching, a man needed one friend who could pull him back up when things went wrong. It was always assumed that James was that friend and vice versa. However, the years since State had proven otherwise to some respect. Angela hoped and prayed the dark times were over for her husband.

One evening, she got a call from Eric after he'd just visited a school. He was recruiting one of the top football players in South Carolina – a kid named Justin Woodberry. Justin was an unbelievable talent being sought by all the big boys in college football. Eric was so hyped that he e-mailed Angela—as if she was a colleague—with his notes about Justin after having reviewed game film with his high school coaches:

"Woodberry can run, close and hit as good as some of the top linebackers in this class. His frame is very impressive and hints of great upside. Long, rangy and his leaner body should explode with bulk when he enters a full-time college weight training program. Baby, this kid could possibly play all three linebacker positions in a 4-3 defense. Justin has great lateral agility and fluidity reminiscent of a young Clump Taylor. I am so excited because he changes direction without a lot of wasted motion and flashes great outside run support skills with his speed and striking closing burst. He is FAST! The one drawback would be his ability to navigate traffic and hold his base at the point of attack versus bigger college linemen on the cutoff block. Has long arms and gets over blocks quickly but does lack a wide base and thickness through his elongated body. HE WILL SEE THE FIELD AS A FROSH!"

As Eric's first recruit, Justin also presented the first instance for Eric of race playing a role in coaching as was discussed in Miami. Justin's parents wanted him to play for an African-American head football coach, which gave Western Ohio an edge. Eric told Angela that his job was to prime Justin and his family so that Coach Davis could come in and close the deal; therefore, he scheduled the visit so that Coach Davis would fly in and show up at Justin's home near the end of the day.

After accompanying the Woodberry's to Justin's basketball game, Eric excused himself informing Mr. Woodberry that he would be back before the end of the game. Just as he turned to leave, Justin grabbed a rebound and made the outlet pass to the guard on the left. Justin sprinted down the right sideline angling towards the middle upon reaching the three-point line. Manuel Herrera, a talent in his own right—rumored to be a viable candidate for the Puerto Rican Olympic team spotted Justin and tossed a lob pass to the rim from half-court. The crowd lurched forward in anticipation as Justin launched himself at the pass. The crowd erupted and Eric dropped his keys as Justin received the pass on the left side of the rim and completed a one-hundred-eighty-degree spin in midair, FLUSHING the basketball on the right side. Justin pointed to his parents.

In unison, Mr. Woodberry and Eric yelled, "THAT'S MY BOY!!" Realizing what had just taken place, Ms. Woodberry elbowed her husband while Eric stood blushing. Mr. Woodberry handed Eric his keys and hugged him. Eric thought to himself, "We got him, he's gonna commit." With that, Eric turned to leave and jump shot making a three-point basket from deep in the corner in excitement. This time, Justin gave an emphatic fist pump and then turned to point with both index fingers to someone on the baseline as he backpedaled into defensive position. To Eric's shock, it was a smiling Coach JR. Eric thought, "what the fudge?!"

Rather than leave, Eric called Coach Davis informing him about the Woodberry family as Coach Davis changed plans and rented a car. Coach Davis made it just as the game ended. Mr. Woodberry invited the coaches back to the house for dinner. Ms. Woodberry made Orange Roughy and vegetables. She had actually left at the start of the fourth quarter with Sommerville High ahead comfortably, led by Justin, who was on his way to dropping fifty.

Justin texted his Dad that he would meet them at the house just before dinner. Mr. Woodberry relayed the information to Coach Davis and Eric. Upon hearing the news, Eric's heart rate quickened. As the two coaches made it to the Woodberry's house, they were surprised to see Eric's former roommate walk out of the door. It appeared that James had made a home visit before Western Ohio could get there. Eric wondered what James was doing, because according to Justin's text, he wasn't due home for another half hour. Eric wanted to be early so he could give Coach Davis the layout of his recruiting plan and time to prepare to "close" Justin.

As James made it down the steps, he stopped by the car to speak to his recruiting adversary and friend.

"What's up, Eric?" James smiled.

"Nothing much," Eric replied. "I didn't know you were recruiting Justin. He's never mentioned Bankhead."

"Well, we were late deciding to recruit Justin, so now we can't let him get away."

Eric retorted, "Not with that All-American running back y'all already have!"

"Oh, we'll see."

Coach Davis hadn't said anything during their exchange, but he finally interrupted. "Hi, I'm Coach Davis, the head coach at Western Ohio. And you are?"

"I'm sorry, Coach," Eric said. "This is Coach James Leaf of Bankhead in Georgia. He's my old college roommate. We were grad assistants together at State University."

"Oh, okay," John smiled. "Now I can see why you two are so competitive."

"It's nice to meet you," James said. "You have to excuse me and Eric, we've been battling since our days as roomies". Eric asked James if Justin and his mother were home. James replied, "Not Justin. I'll see you later, my job is done here! I have another kid to visit."

"Are you sure, man?" Eric blurted out. "Is it the athlete you're visiting, or their mothers?"

"Hey, hey – don't you act holier-than-thou with me! I know you, Eric," said James while adjusting his tie and shirt collar. Meanwhile, Ms. Woodberry was peeking at the scene from behind her Venetian Blinds.

As James pulled away in his car, Coach Davis asked what that was all about. Eric responded, "We have a love-hate relationship. Everything we do has become a competition. Besides, I don't want him to beat us on Justin since I know he'll pull out all the stops."

"Wait, are you suggesting …" Coach Davis started to ask as Eric cut in, "I'm just saying Coach, he was called the "Beast" at State and a lesser known fact was that some of the coaching staff and his professors labeled him "Shortcut." James always seemed to find a way to make things happen.

As the two coaches waited for Justin, his stepfather arrived and invited them in. What ensued was a general conversation between the parents and the coaches about what recruiting was like before the NCAA stepped in with all these crazy rules.

"Eric, you're lucky. When I started coaching in the 1980's, recruiting was really different. I was once told by a high school coach that their "Niggras" don't go to the school where I was coaching. That particular coach was a prick and I never went back. It was also a time when every big school had their own 'suitcase coach' that came in to seal the deal."

"What's a suitcase coach?"

"That's a duffle bag boy, the coach who made the payments to the athletes," John explained. "That coach had the confidence of the head coach, so if anything happened, he'd take the fall for the head coach. In return, he would be protected and got to spend hand-to-hand time with major boosters who would make sure he was well-paid under the table. Sometimes, it's the players that sink the ship. Coach Davis recounted a story of a promising young talent from North Houston's Forestbrook High School. The young man was a quarterback, which was intriguing for, this time, the mid-1980s because assuredly any athletic quarterback from the inner-city would be converted to defensive back, runningback, linebacker, in college. They were essentially destined to play anything but quarterback in college. But this kid, Chris was special. Coach Davis didn't mention his name out of respect for the kid's privacy. At the time, Forestbrook was a juggernaut averaging sixty points per game. Chris was throwing for 500 yards here, six touchdowns there, at a time when running the ball was prominent all over the country. It wasn't that way in Texas. With the advent of the Run-n-Shoot offenses of the University of Houston, the then Houston Gamblers of the USFL, and later the NFL's Oilers, the Greater Houston area was the epicenter of the spread offense passing game. But, this kid Chris, everyone wanted him. He had his hands out and grabbing as much "swag (stuff we all get)" as he could. Here's the kicker—a testament to how the "recruiting machine" can destroy a person. It was the week of big regional semi-final playoff game with Forestbrook going against another top-team from Houston—Lamar. Following the Wednesday practice, Chris is being interviewed live by a local reporter. They went through the usual gamut of questions about the game then the reporter asked the main question:

"Chris, everyone wants to know. Have you made a decision on where you'll play college football next year? Texas, Southern Cal, Notre Dame? I know it's tough for you…"

The kid's response was tragic: "It's simple. I'm going to the whatever school pays me the most."

This was live television. The reporter was stunned and before young Chris made it home for dinner, he had no future in college football and several major universities had investigations launched against them by the NCAA over their recruitment of Chris. So, there is definitely a fine line in recruiting that some schools don't mind crossing.

"Also, coaches would hide recruits back then," Coach Davis went on. "Imagine that you're my recruit, and I came to your house the day before signing. I'd hide you in a hotel under a false name and take you to school the next morning so you could sign your letter of intent." Mr. Woodberry offered his two cents, "I remember hearing a story about a wild ass coach that actually spent the night on a dirt floor of a recruit's house in some obscure little town in Texas. Each time a different coach would knock on the door, he would answer it!"

Continuing, Coach Davis stated, "This was a different time, and it had to change. I can remember spending the night in front of a recruit's house along with two other coaches from two different schools so that they wouldn't take the kid and hide him before the 8:00 a.m. contact time! Believe me, times have changed!"

"This was the death of the Southwest Conference," John explained. "I know you're too young to remember that conference Eric, but it had no checks and balances." As he finished his statement, he and Eric saw Justin pull up with his girlfriend. "Don't mention your friend being here. That's up to Justin's mother to tell."

"How are you doing, Justin?" the head coach said as he got out of the car. "How are you, young lady?" Eric chimed in "Coach, I see why Justin stayed a little longer. Who wants to speak with coaches when you've got better things to attend to." They all laughed and headed into the house.

Justin said he was fine, and then his stepfather said, "By the way, my name is Grant. Michael Grant. Please, just call me Michael." Coach Davis was a little dumbfounded. He didn't like for his coaches to make those kinds of mistakes; he believed that he should know everything about a family. Eric knew he'd made a big mistake, but he kept on going.

As they made it to the door, Eric asked Justin, "How do you feel about your big game tonight?"

"Great!" Justin responded. "We just beat our biggest rival."

"Good," Coach Davis pitched in. "Glad to see you standout in such a big game." As they entered the house, the coaches saw Justin's mother walk into the room. "Mrs. Grant, how are doing?" Coach Davis introduced himself. "It's nice to meet you."

"My name is Woodberry," Justin's mother stated. "We're not married." At that point, the head coach felt stupid. This was information he should have already known! He apologized for the error, and Ms. Woodberry told him it was a common assumption. She was a nice woman, and one could tell she used to be very beautiful. However, forty-five years and five kids had taken their toll on her. Justin was the middle child, and he had two younger brothers aged nine and five respectively.

After some small talk, Coach Davis got down to business, and you could tell he was an old pro at recruiting. He started breaking down to Mr. Grant and Ms. Woodberry what Western Ohio had to offer their son. "We don't make promises about you being a starter, nor that you will play as a freshman," he told Justin. "You'll have to come and compete for a position. The best players will play. The advantages you have are that you are an excellent student, you are extremely athletic, and can run really well. Those factors typically translate into playing early." He also told them about what the school had to offer as far as education emphasizing the Chemical Engineering program based upon Eric's research. One good thing that Eric had accomplished was establishing a relationship with some of Justin's instructors. Thus, Coach Davis had a good idea that Justin would be able to handle the transition from high school to college in terms of academics and what types of majors Justin had shown interest in the past.

Once he was finished, Ms. Woodberry nodded and said, "It sounds good. When can we visit?"

"Can you come next week?"

"We're going to Florida State, and then we have two visits left. One of those will be Western Ohio" Ms. Woodberry said. "Then I want him to visit Bankhead."

Justin looked over and said, "Oh, Okay. I'll visit you at Western Ohio in two weeks."

Ms. Woodberry announced that it was time to eat. Coach Davis, the old pro, jumped in and said, "What are we having?" Eric tried to look enthused, though he noticed that Justin's family lived in a double-wide trailer that wasn't very clean. Also, he was a vegan. He didn't want to look odd or impolite, however, so he made himself finish dinner. Surprisingly, he liked the fish.

As Coach Davis and he left for the evening, Eric did not say much. About a mile up the road, he pulled over and threw up. It had been a bad day for him at every turn – he'd been unprepared and had made too many mistakes. Coach Davis knew Eric wasn't feeling well, so he told him to just get him to the airport, and that they would talk in the office during the weekend recruiting activity.

Two weeks flew by, and Eric really improved upon his recruiting of Justin. The fact Coach Davis was an African American, however, was not enough to convince Justin to give a verbal commitment to sign with them. During the weekend of the young player's visit, Western Ohio only had five recruits visiting, so they could really spend time with Justin.

All the graduate assistants arrived at the R.L. Session Athletic Center at about 4:00 p.m. just as Justin and his mother showed up. The NCAA rules did not allow Western to pay for Mr. Grant because he was considered a family friend. Interestingly, Ms. Woodberry, a petite woman standing perhaps 5' was wearing a Western Ohio basketball jersey as a dress. Eric thought that maybe this was an omen.

While there, Eric talked to Justin about the district championship game against Anderson—a perennial state power that took place during Justin's junior season. He told the young man that his exploits during his senior year and his performances on the basketball court had solidified his status as an elite prospect. Last season's district championship game was Justin's coming out party.

In the game Justin had 19 solo tackles, 22 overall including 3 sacks and 6 hurries; Justin rushed for 103 yards and one touchdown on 8 carries. He returned an interception 67 yards for a touchdown; and finally, in a dazzling exhibition of agility, vision, power, and speed Justin fielded a punt just outside the numbers on the 11-yard line, took it all the way to the opposite sideline and sprinted to the end-zone for the game-winning touchdown. This kid was special. So it was no surprise to see that type of athleticism on display two weeks before the visit. It was clear that Justin had a great game, and that Justin had really put on a good show for the many coaches in the stands watching. Everyone wanted this kid. College Football Nation now ranked him as the number 5 overall recruit in the nation.

As he finished telling Justin about the weekend schedule, the young man's host walked in. Juan Meadows was hand-picked by Coach Davis. He was the clean-up host – he had a 92% sign rate and was now facing his biggest challenge at Western. Eric advised Juan to be safe.

"Don't worry," Juan replied. "I have the perfect girl for him to freak. She'll make his toes curl!"

"I don't want to know about the night!" Eric insisted.

After Justin left with Juan, Ms. Woodberry asked Eric to give her a ride back to the hotel. As they arrived at the Hyatt, she asked him to come in so that she could discuss the offer with him. "No problem," Eric replied.

While inside Ms. Woodberry's hotel suite, things quickly started to change. She told Eric to call her Betty and asked if it would be okay if she had a drink. She opened up the suite's bar. To Eric, it was evident that this woman was very familiar with spirits, aperitifs, and all the rest of it. Eric tried to get into his sales pitch, but Betty was not interested in hearing about Western Ohio. The more she drank, the more suggestive she became. She grabbed a pillow off the couch, pretending it was a football, and got into an offensive center position. She asked Eric to play quarterback. Unwittingly, Eric walked over and saw that she was wearing only a red G-string under her Western Ohio dress. After snapping the "ball" Betty ran a pass route to the couch, Eric lobbed a pass which Betty dove onto the couch to catch. Landing in the corner of the couch Betty's legs were opened like a book as she tried to get up. She tossed the pillow back to Eric as he clicked on her laptop on the table. After a few mouse clicks, the room was filled with the seductive music of R. Kelly, the song was "It Seems Like You're Ready."

"Toss me the ball, Coach."

Eric obliged. Upon catching the pillow, Betty challenged Eric to stop her from scoring. "The touchdown is the couch, see if you can stop me," she giggled after downing a little bottle of Hennessey. Not really knowing what was happening, Eric softly "wrapped" Betty up and she promptly fell onto the couch with Eric ending up on top of her. Next thing Eric knew Betty tried to kiss him. Like he'd been backed up into the red zone, he was stunned. At first, he responded to her advances. Her kisses were soft and she smelled great, she was a temptress in every sense. As Eric returned her kisses, Betty began to tug at his shirt, and his right hand cupped her breast. Betty was becoming more aggressive, unfastening Eric's belt while his right hand was now at the "Y."

Eric was becoming aroused and Betty's roving hands knew it. But Eric's mind was racing and he began thinking about his young family. Pulling away abruptly, Eric told Betty that he had to leave. She was not happy. This woman was a freak, and Eric simply could not do "it" for the team. It became apparent to him that this decision would have far reaching implications for his future—both short and long term. He knew deep in his gut that his friend "the Beast" had definitely laid down with this woman. He then began to think about how common this type of thing was on the recruiting trail. Where did he fall? Was he typical or atypical?

Once he made it home, Eric got undressed and took a shower. He walked into the bedroom just stared at his wife while she slept. He knew that with all that he had put Angela through, cheating on her was not an option. Nevertheless, his suspicions about James' and Ms. Woodberry's relationship were mounting the more that Eric considered what had taken place in South

Carolina. His morning conversations with James began to confirm the relationship. James was simply too non-committal about Bankhead's interest in Justin. James didn't believe he would give Bankhead a verbal, which was bullshit in Eric's mind. Bankhead was on par with Florida State, LSU, Alabama, and so on. Eric had never heard James so pessimistic about anything, now he wasn't sure about the prospects of landing a top recruit? Eric smelled something rotten in Denmark. In Eric's mind, James was definitely banging "Betty Boop."

After the recruiting weekend ended, Coach Davis asked Eric to take Justin and his mother to the airport. Eric never brought up what had happened. After arriving at the airport, Eric asked Justin if he'd enjoyed himself.

Justin smiled wildly because his mind was still tripping off the "experience" that Juan planned for him—Quietly, he'd hoped that nobody heard him screaming in ecstasy.

Justin said that he had. Right then, Ms. Woodberry cut in. "I really didn't enjoy myself," she sneered. "We'll let you know our decision."

After Eric made it back to the office, his head coach called him into the office to tell him he really felt like they might have sealed the deal with this weekend's visits. He went on to tell Eric how good a job he had done rebounding from his shaky start. Eric didn't feel as good about the weekend, but he never told anyone about what happened that night at the hotel. He knew that it would be an uphill battle to beat Bankhead because Bankhead had the last crack at Justin and his mother.

One week before the signing date, Justin Woodberry held a press conference to announce his college intentions. Eric was not going to be surprised. Justin chose Bankhead University, and that confirmed that James Leaf was now a major recruiter in college football. Now Eric was left with a bunch of questions from Coach Davis about what had happened with the "can't-miss" recruit.

Eric spent one season as wide receivers coach, and as fate would have it, defensive coordinator Coach Phil Moran accepted an offer to coach professional football. Coach Moran was the elder statesmen on Coach Davis' staff. Coach Davis had built a staff of young coaches whom he perceived as being more energetic. Now he had a hiring decision to make since Coach Moran was leaving. Eric believed that he was the man for the job and would be a great fit as defensive coordinator since he felt really comfortable with Coach Davis. Again, it was Angela who came to her husband's rescue because she was fed up with hearing her husband talk about the opening for five straight days. She'd had enough.

"Damn, baby," Angela said, "if you want this position, just ask for it. If you don't want it, please don't bring it up again!" Angela was frustrated with Eric's lack of confidence. Coaching was something that he wanted, but sometimes it appeared as if he was incapable of fighting for himself. This was something that really pissed Angela off. Eric did not realize that she was beginning to perceive him as weak. This exchange was her way of telling him to "man up."

"What's that phrase that James always used in school? You gotta hang or something?"

"The Beast stole that catch-phrase from John Manning. It was 'you gotta let you nuts hang,'" replied an agitated Eric.

"Right, that's what I am saying, baby. No matter what happens, 'you gotta let it all hang out'. Just go for it already, shit!"

"Well, it's not that easy since I'm the last person Coach Davis hired, and I'm on the offensive side of the ball right now," Eric replied.

"But, who really gives a shit! Quit making excuses. It's still football, right?"

Instinctively, Eric advised Angela to get a grip on her tone. Nevertheless, Eric sat and thought for a moment. His wife had a point. He had to muster up the courage to ask his boss for the opportunity to be the defensive coordinator.

After one of Coach Davis's very common marathon staff meetings — Coach Davis felt it was important to work long hours to keep the young coaches out of trouble and to cover everything daily—Eric declared, "I'm applying for the defensive coordinator position."

"All right," Coach Davis replied, "but you need to know I have someone in mind already."

Eric wanted to leave it alone, but he knew that he couldn't face his wife if he didn't stand up for his chance. "But coach," he blurted, "can you just give me thirty minutes of your time? It won't cost anything!"

"Damn it, I know!" Coach Davis said, irritated. Two hours later, the coach allowed Eric into his office. With no written speech, Eric's thoughts were so thorough and precise that Coach was definitely impressed.

Coach Davis had offered the job to long-time friend Mark Evans, who was Coach Davis's defensive coordinator during his time as a student-athlete. The reason Coach Evans hadn't yet accepted the position was that he wanted to retire after 35 years of coaching. To Eric's benefit, Coach Davis didn't have a back-up plan. Eric's persistence gave him one.

Following the meeting, Coach Davis invited Eric down to the field. This was Western Ohio's "Pro Day." In all the excitement, Eric had simply forgotten about the event. This was the day that all seniors and underclassmen having declared for the NFL Draft workout for pro scouts. This is possibly the best opportunity for a player to show his wares because he is in a comfortable environment. The player is surrounded by his college coaches and teammates. The coaches only run the drills which show the players in their best light. In short, the workout is setup for the players to look good. Interestingly enough, it is also an opportunity for the coaches to try to show their skills—hoping one day to make the leap to the NFL themselves (in any capacity).

The player of note at the workout was Montego Ballard, Western Ohio's career leader in receptions, yards, touchdowns, and kick returns for touchdowns. This was an amazing feat considering that the young man was a partial qualifier—meaning he was ineligible to play as a freshman. Additionally, Montego had overcome a bout with a form of Hodgkin's lymphoma as a sophomore. Thus, in two seasons, every career receiving record known to Western Ohio had been obliterated by this Hollywood-ready "comeback kid."

The workouts were largely underwhelming for the most part. Montego was scheduled to perform in the middle of the session. There was a buzz when he walked into the practice bubble. Montego was so excited. He had gone out to the mall to get some workout gear. He had the latest dri-fit shorts and form-fitting tee. Accompanying Montego was Ray Jackson, a local consultant specializing in route running. Montego's agent hired Mr. Jackson to help Montego get in and out of cuts for the scouts. Ray would throw passes to Montego at the workout. Ray was riddled with intricate tattoos and wore oversized clothing as a rule. Ray was 33 years old and had been consulting with pro quarterback, receiver, and defensive back prospects since he was 22. He was self-made and didn't care about his appearance. His performance and the success of his clients spoke volumes.

Montego was a shredded and physically imposing figure at 6'4" 220 lbs. His favorite team was the San Francisco 49ers. He was decked out in 49er red—no logo (not wanting to show partiality for sure). He was flaming red: shoes, no socks, shorts, tee emblazoned with the number "2", bandana, sweatbands—Montego was clean. His outfit matched his nickname: "Prime

Time." As he walked up to begin the workout, there was a buzz in the bubble: "Prime Time, Prime Time, Prime Time." People began chanting his name.

A few of the scouts began to scoff as he walked in. Many were furiously scribbling in their notepads. But it was the action of the scouts during the workout that told the story. Montego was never a burner but ran a decent, low 4.5 second in the 40-yard dash. He ran all the standard routes, no balls touched the ground. Montego was in and out of breaks clean. Montego also showed that he could work against press coverage and get depth quickly. None of this seemed to matter. Eric noticed and nudged Coach Davis that the scouts stopped taking notes on Montego. Something had gone wrong during the workout.

Montego felt that his workout had solidified him as an early second-round pick, if not a late first round selection. Following the workout, the scouts were non-committal. There was a consensus brewing that Montego was gang-affiliated. Where had the scouts gotten that notion? Montego was implicated and cleared of an on-campus break-in during the season. This was all part of the public record. Could it have been his attire? Again, anyone who knew him knew of his love for the 49ers. In interviews, Montego frequently credits his hours of film study on Jerry Rice for his on-field success. This kid was anything but a gang-member. He came from a middle-class, two-parent family in Cameron, Texas. He was a Dean's List student, majoring in Pre-Med. Something had gone completely wrong. Coach Charley always said that if you could play, the NFL would find you. "Talent trumps all," Coach Charley would say. Coaches ask themselves, "Can this guy help us win?" If the answer is "yes" nothing else matters.

Montego's agent still could never get a read on his draft stock. He could not find out what had occurred at the workout. Montego's stock had plummeted off the chart. The NFL Draft—Day One came and went. Day Two was a nightmare. Montego Ballard, Western Ohio's career leader in all relevant receiver statistics was neither drafted nor invited to any camp as a free agent. This all took place because he was labeled a gang member by someone influential at Western's Pro Day. This was a terrible day. Eric wondered aloud how this could have happened to such a good guy.

8 CONFERENCE

After six seasons as a major football coach, James had hit a wall in his career. He'd never been considered for a coordinator position, and he had never been asked to apply for one during his time at Bankhead. The team had been very successful during his tenure thus far. There were six-(6) consecutive bowl appearances, three-(3) New Year's Day bowls, and one-(1) BCS bowl appearance. However, the publicity and notoriety that flows with this level of success never trickled down to James because he was only a position coach, but recognized nationally as a master recruiter. James just hadn't run anything yet. This was beginning to piss James off. Eric had enjoyed coordinating duties albeit while working for also-rans. James was doing fine, but he simply hadn't stood out. He hadn't protected his spot nor given his boss a reason to keep him. The upcoming World Football Coaches Association Convention would be of the highest importance since he was now out of a job.

Behind the scenes, there was more going on at Bankhead. Following James' fifth season, Coach Manavich shook up the staff. He brought in a new defensive coordinator from Fort Worth University in Texas. The coach's name was Johnny "Rat" Henderson. Players called him Coach Henderson or Coach Hen. Fellow coaches called him "JH" professionally; however, on the Bankhead staff, he was known as "Rat." This was a dirty, ambitious, cut-throat "sum-bitch." Everything that happened with James' ouster was no accident; however, James served as the smoke screen. Six weeks into the following season, Coach Manavich himself was shown the door. What follows is how it all went down because it was more than just James' issues with women.

James didn't feel he had done anything wrong. Coach Manavich told him that his termination was due to a need for change in staff, and the fact that the running backs were no longer responding to him as a coach. The crazy part about Coach Manavich's statement was that James's last two running backs were in the NFL. The truth of the matter was that James had yet to mature, and Coach Manavich had to preserve his staff's unity. James was still reluctant to attend meetings on time. James spent most of his time in and about the local social scene as opposed to being in the film room helping with offensive game plans and pass protections. James' players were talented, but they were beginning to play a selfish brand of football. Coach Manavich felt that the other coaches would have revolted if he kept James. Coach Manavich was caught between a rock and a hard place but kindheartedly allowed James to resign instead of firing him.

I just can't get past how Rat Henderson orchestrated the Bankhead implosion. During his first meeting with the rest of the staff—I mean as Coach Manavich was introducing him—Rat Henderson was sizing up the men in the room. This included Coach Manavich. From this very meeting, despite all the success that Bankhead had experienced, this was a staff in flux, a program on the brink of collapse. Coach Manavich had become a media hound and had left the majority of the day to day staff administration to Jim Butler and Bumpy Walters—the defensive backs and offensive coordinator, respectively. What was the glue that held this staff together? How was Bankhead still winning?

The answer was simple—it's always simple. Bankhead was still winning because of the recruits. You show me a great coach and I'll show you a host of damn good players. James was jockeying for more control with recruiting. He actually wanted to become the recruiting coordinator but didn't really know how to do it. He sought out Eric's assistance; however, after the Woodberry situation, Eric simply wasn't inclined to help James. Due to Angela's influence, Eric played the role and offered some shallow, useless advice which James rightly ignored.

Rat's deconstruction of the staff was systematic. A model case of divide and conquer. James was the youngest, most inexperienced coach on the staff; therefore, he was ripe for the picking. One particular week, Bankhead was scheduled to play a rival—Florida Tech. This team was known for blitzing and playing man coverage. Rat was an architect of the defense Florida Tech was running—having served on the same staff as Marty Weeks, Florida Tech's DC on the Pittsburgh Steelers staff in the early 1990s.

At Rat's suggestion, Coach Manavich designated that Rat coordinate the "blitz pickup" period of the Tuesday and Wednesday practice. Rat diagrammed the blitz tendencies and packages based upon the Bankhead's game plan for the week. In theory, Bankhead would attack the defense based upon known fronts and coverages that would be utilized to defend them. According to Rat, he trained Coach Weeks in the defense that Florida Tech is running. He knew what Tech would do based upon down, distance, and field position. What Rat also knew was that James was not a huge proponent of film study. "James, make sure that you let your guys know that when we motion to that open set, the defensive adjustment will be linebackers through the A-gap to our left." The plan was for the back to "scan protect inside out to the left" with the quarterback on a half-roll left out of the shotgun away from the free rusher. This appeared to be a fundamentally sound plan.

During the practices, the James coached his runningbacks to make the blitz pickup adjustments based upon the diagrams Rat provided. The youngsters did fine, with a couple of busted assignments on Tuesday, but none on Wednesday. During film study of practice among the coordinators and Coach Manavich, Rat planted the seed. "Coach, it's clear that we can spread these guys out. I just don't know if our backs are sure about where they fit during blitz pickup. They even appear to be tipping the protection pre-snap. James is aware of the protection plan isn't he?" Coach Manavich listened intently and watched the "Blitz Period" portion of practice for another twenty minutes. He thought that the backs would be okay. Rat continued, "Let's face it. This kid has coached on his name from State U. He has no real sense of technique. He's not a coach." Coach Manavich had heard enough. Rat would not relent. "You mark my words, his laissez-faire, nonchalant, "shuck and jive" coaching routine is going to get someone hurt, or worse yet, cost us a damn ballgame."

James' immaturity was evident at the resignation party, hosted at Coach Manavich's house. After dinner and the end-of-the-year toast, Coach Dean Steinbach went looking for his wife, Kirsten. She was nowhere to be found. Coach Steinbach was instantly panicked inside.

Coach Steinbach was a reserved and a very insecure kind of person. He always thought that the opposing team was stealing our signals; or that we had spies in the stadium during closed practices; furthermore, he always kissed Coach Manavich's ass and fished for compliments and confirmation that he was doing a good job. This guy was a masterful tactician in football terms, but a total wreck as a man. This seeped over into his personal life as well. He was driven by the perceived notion that he was a better coach than the other coaches since he had never been a player of the game.

For the past year, Coach Steinbach and his wife Kirsten had been a little distant from each other. He thought it was just one of those marriage stages all couples went through. The two of them had been together for over fifteen years and had weathered several major storms in their relationship. This time, it felt different for Dean. He could sense that something was wrong. When he finally found his wife, he found more than what he wanted to see. From the porch, Dean could see that his windows were foggy. With the available moonlight, Dean could see a silhouette. He thought to himself, "Whew, she's just getting something out of the car." So, Dean continued towards the car but began to have nauseous feeling in the pit of his stomach, a percolating sense of dread. He could now tell that there was more than one person in the car, the doors were closed as well.

Upon his arrival to the car door, Dean abruptly opened the door to the Lexus LS 450 and found his beloved wife engaged in fellatio with James in the back seat.

"Why?" Dean shouted at James, screaming at the top of his lungs. "Why? You're supposed to be my friend! My colleague! I tried to help your career you dirty sum-bitch!" The look of disappointment, disbelief, and flat-out anger on his face was unmistakable as Kirsten and James tried to scramble away from one another. Kirsten exited the car defiantly. "Screw you, Dean! Don't get mad now! "Pushing him backward, she continues, "He paid attention to me! You've taken me for granted." Rat chimed in, being held back as he tried to make his way towards the car, "that's right James, you can't be trusted to do anything but screw up! In football and in life you're a screw-up. What do you do—wallow in your misery as a failed coach in the arms of other men's wives? Bankhead hasn't been shit since that debacle with Florida Tech. You cost us a bowl bid, asshole." Rat tried to make his way over to James, but James was busy with Dean.

Returning his ire to James, Dean yelled, "I confided in you! I trusted you! And you'd do this to me? Go and screw my wife?! I'm going to kill you!" The shouting and commotion brought out the rest of the party and the neighbors. Completely out of control, Dean grabbed a brick from the Manaviches' garden and went after James. Still possessing the remarkable quickness that made him an escape artist in college was on display. "Feet don't fail me now!" crossed his mind as Dean charged.

Meanwhile, Coach Manavich thought back to the Florida Tech game. It was truly an offensive embarrassment. Having shut down Bankhead's daunting rushing attack, Florida Tech set its sights on shutting down the passing game. As expected Bankhead tried to spread the field, Florida Tech countered with a barrage of complex blitzes. The salient point is that these schemes used by Florida Tech were tendency breakers. The veteran Bankhead offensive line adjusted; however, the noticeable weak link in the protection was the backs. They were drilled all week that the blitz would come from the inside. The protection scheme was "scan inside out." The linebackers never came. They would show blitz and drop out wide or buzz into the curl zones. The quarterback was sacked eleven times. On eight of these sacks, the backs never touched a defender.

While having another drink, Coach Manavich recalled the exchange during the coaches' meeting. This footage was painful to watch. James had yet to arrive at the meeting. He was just arriving at the airport after a recruiting visit. The offense went three and out on its first four drives of the game. On one drive, the Tech defense registered two sacks and one deflection. Rat was whispering to other coaches in the background. Through the session, the whispers became murmurs.

Almost on cue, as James walked into the meeting, Rat was in mid-sentence, "Coach the runningbacks have no clue what the game-plan was going in." James' response was immediate.

"That's bullshit. You are the defensive scheme guru, the protection plan was designed essentially by you based upon your knowledge of the system we faced."

"I would expect you to shift blame for your piss-poor coaching," said Rat. Turning his attention to Coach Manavich, Rat said, "roll the tape back for him, show him the cutups from the open set." James had no idea what was about to occur. By responding to the criticism with anger and indifference, he had dignified Rat and fallen into his trap.

Coach Manavich ran the series of plays back over and over and over. Sack after sack after sack, finally asking, "what's going on here, James?" Rat went further, "just what in the hell are you teaching these kids?" These were not words any coach wanted to hear. This was an outright statement before the entire staff that James didn't know what the hell he was doing. The final play of the open set cutups showed Bankhead's senior quarterback Cory Bonner, being carted off the field. He was the recipient of a devastating frontside hit. The backs dove inside to pickup blitzes that did not come, leaving Cory open for punishment.

Rat began throwing aside desks at the site of Bonner. Rat was trying to get at James, who did not move during this fracas. Rat raised his hands to swing. At the advance, James simply craned on one leg and kicked the dog-shit out of Rat. I mean, he hit him right square in the jaw. More than anything, this act sealed his fate at Bankhead.

With Kirsten circling and James running out of room to run due to the gathering crowd, James strafed to his left and squared off on a charging Dean near the entrance to the Manavichs' home. The Bankhead coaching staff would have been going to a funeral if Kirsten had not stepped between the two men. She might have been a cheat, but she was also a brave woman. With Dean charging and aiming with the brick, James was bracing to "shoot his ankles" and dump him. But Kirsten was charging, too. "Dean, don't you touch him!" As she yelled this, she launched herself at Dean and goat-roped him forcing him into the hedge bushes. Kirsten, an All-American striker with Penn State, single-handedly stopped her husband from murdering two people that night – James and herself. The scene was something like one from the Jerry Springer Show.

Many at the party were surprised at the love affair. Coach Terry Martin told his wife, Shelia, that he would never have suspected anything between Coach JR and Coach Steinbach's wife. To Terry's surprise, his wife already knew. Why is it that women always know? Is it the estrogen?

"All the coaches' wives have known for months that Kirsten and James were seeing each other; apparently he's a great boyfriend—at least according to the reports Kirsten and others around campus have given." Shelia confessed to her husband, confronting his shocked and dumbfounded look. "Baby, it takes a strong woman to put up with an insecure man like Dean. Kirsten was fed up and wanted some attention. It didn't matter where or from whom she got it." Sheila dropped another bombshell about the fact that the pregnancy that Kirsten miscarried last year was definitely James' child. Coach Martin's blood began to boil. Had James possibly touched his wife?

This situation that Coach Dean went through reminds me of a lesson that I learned early from an uncle while in middle school. Uncle Roy Lee told me, "Nephew, if you do it right, it don't cost nothing to pay a woman some attention. But know this, if you don't pay her attention now, it could cost you everything later." Tell me that ain't some of the realest wisdom a man ever spit. It seems that Coach Dean learned that lesson the hard way.

***

James and his college roommate seemed to be headed in different directions. Even though he was considered one of the best recruiters in the country, it was not a good year for James to be seeking employment. He realized that his trip to the World Football Coaches Association Convention in Houston that year was going to be strictly a business trip to find a job. Eric, on the other hand, had rebounded from last year's shaky start in Division I-A football to become a successful defensive coordinator. Eric's hard work earned a top twenty posting for total defense – the first such place for the university in fifty years. He was selected as a keynote speaker at the convention that year. He chose the topic, "The Western Ohio University Way of Defense." It was a huge honor for him. He started to prepare for his presentation at the convention like he was getting ready to take the bar exam.

Because of the birth of their second child, Erica – a beautiful little girl named after her father – Angela said that she would not make it to that year's convention. Coaching conventions were all about testosterone, and she preferred a different atmosphere. What she didn't have the heart to tell her husband was that she actually hated the conventions—despite finding her husband a good job at a convention years earlier. It was because of this fact that Eric insisted that she should come this year.

By chance, both James and Eric happened to be staying at the Wyndham Hotel in downtown Houston. As Eric was checking in, he noticed James in the lobby and went over to speak. He had no idea that James was out of a job since everyone at Bankhead did an excellent job of suppressing the incident.

"Hey!" Eric greeted his friend cheerfully. "How are things, James?"

"Things are going okay," James muttered in reply.

"Where's the staff? Did you all fly in separately?"

"Well, yeah, I flew in separate from the staff. But that's because I got fired. They're staying at the Hilton."

Stunned and empathetic, Eric asked, "Fired? For what? You were their best recruiter! Their clean-up guy! You were the man!" They walk towards the hotel lounge and grab a table. James has still been reluctant to recount the facts behind his firing. Eric continues to brainstorm and asked again, "How do you fire 'Mariano Rivera?' it just doesn't make any sense...unless you did something." Before James could even answer, a realization popped into Eric's head. "Hold up. Who did you screw? James, I know you. You got a bad habit of putting that thing between your legs in the wrong place. Was it the vice president's wife or some administrator on campus?"

James tried to act hurt. "Hey, what's up with that, man? You know it was nothing like that! Coach Manavich just told me that he wanted to go in a different direction, that's all."

"Yeah, if you say so," Eric replied, not believing a word. "You know I'll find out eventually. I just feel like you owe me the truth."

"Look, I don't want to talk about Bankhead. Tell me what jobs you heard were open."

"I don't know, man. I haven't been looking for jobs, but now I have a reason to keep my ears open." He cracked a smile, trying to cheer up his friend. "You're the big-time recruiter. You won't have any problem finding another job. Especially since every Division I-A coach here wants a clean-up hitter!" Eric was only teasing, but James didn't take it well. He knew deep down that Coach Manavich was going to put the word out about him screwing another coach's wife. He knew he would have to beat Coach Manavich to the punch.

More than anything, Coach Manavich was also bitter at his naïveté. Rat had bitten him in the ass as well. Remember, shortly after James' outster, Manavich was on the way out the door. Rat had been having closed door meetings with the Bankhead Athletic Director three weeks before the Florida Tech game. He raised issues about the staff being full of renegades; that Manavich had lost control of the program and employed no institutional control. Bankhead, according to Rat, was ripe for severe NCAA sanctions without proper direction.

Eric checked into his room at the Wyndham Hotel and called Angela to see how she and the baby were doing. He told her about bumping into James in the lobby, and that James had been fired.

"That's sad," Angela said. "I hate to see James out of work like this."

"Sad??" Eric snapped. "James is a big boy. He was never sad for us when we were out there struggling trying to make it."

"Look baby, you were working, just not where you wanted to be. James is out of work. That's two different things. What happened to him? Bankhead has been doing really good, right?"

"Well, when you're making $30,000 like I was, while he was making over six figures, it's hard to feel sorry." Eric's tone was stern. "James has made his money. I wish you would've felt sorry for us like that." Angela just fell silent, which was an indication to Eric that she did not approve of his tone or attitude. Eric sighed and began to tell the story as he received it from James and two other colleagues on the Bankhead staff.

It appears that there was a cancer on the staff and his name was Rat Henderson. James isn't really sure, but my other two friends are certain that Rat accepted Coach Manavich's offer to become defensive coordinator with the express intent to become head coach of Bankhead within three years. Angela, sipping on green tea, was shocked. "I don't know why you're looking like that. Coaches are no different than anyone else you might meet in an office or boardroom—ambitious and cut-throat. The simple truth is that Rat was playing "chess" while Manavich was playing "checkers." Both have strategy, but one game is played to win, the other is played for fun.

As it turns out, Rat intentionally misdirected the entire staff on the blitz packages that they would face in the Florida Tech game. He offered no suggestions for adjustments during the game or at halftime. Frankly nobody cared to hear his advice at that time. Coach Manavich was busy ripping the entire offensive staff and players a new asshole. He called out James in a meeting, even tried to scrap with him. James drop-kicked him—but that's not how the story came out. Actually, nobody outside the coaches' meeting knew about the fracas. The players definitely didn't know about it. But the situation gets deeper. Rat did not bother to point out that James had made his own adjustments with the protection as far as the runningbacks responsibilities. But the situation gets deeper.

Practice became a joke as game plans were put together to set the team up to fail. Rat began to employ the high-risk aspects of the defensive scheme— trying to disguise coverages and blitz packages, dropping defensive lineman into curls zones. Opposing teams just brought in a second tight end and walked down the field on Bankhead. Bankhead's defense went from 21st in the nation to 109th almost overnight. It was pure sabotage as Rat began to undress all his defensive coaches during the game from the pressbox; following the game in meetings. See, Rat coached linebackers. He allowed his players to "wildcat" in the scheme. Sure, the linebackers made a lot of tackles. The problem is that they didn't make many tackles for loss. These tackles were taking place in the secondary.

The other coaches saw this and coupled with his divisive comments, Rat had succeeded in fracturing the staff. Part of the staff was loyal to Manavich, part was loyal to Henderson, and then there was James—running around fucking all the wives. Not sure if he got Rat's wife—I wouldn't know what to say if he did. "Why," asked Angela only to hear Eric respond that Rat's wife was either a prime candidate for "The Biggest Loser" or was trying to eat her way to the Duke University Diet Center. It is true that James will hit anything, but Eric couldn't imagine James with Rat's "manatee" of a wife.

One game, Rat did not call one defense—he's the defensive coordinator! He claimed to have been fed up with the poor professionalism of his staff and advocated firing two of the key defensive assistants—these were holdovers from the previous coordinator. Manavich kept them on because they knew the scheme that Henderson would bring with him.

Remember that while all this is going on, Rat was having meetings with the Athletic Director almost regularly. He was "pouring salt" on the entire staff. What sealed Manavich was the five losses by double digits where the team simply just found new ways to lose each week. Also, Rat floated a rumor that Coach Manavich was sharing an apartment with a pre-med coed from Dekalb. He allegedly took the moral high road and accused the entire staff of knowing about the inappropriate relationship but remaining silent.

"Sure, it's an unfortunate situation, but as I said, James has made his money. I don't really care that he lost his job or that he couldn't navigate a poisonous, ruinous element on the staff—in many ways, James was just as destructive. To hell with it," exhorted Eric.

The tone of his wife's voice changed then. "Well, the kids are doing fine. I'm glad you asked. You take care, I love you."

Eric knew he had ticked his wife off and said, "I love you too, baby."

After hanging up the phone, Eric started back working on his presentation for the convention, but he was finding it hard to concentrate. There was a knock at the door. It was Coach Davis and Coach Charley, who stopped by to invite him to a private party. Eric wanted to stay and work on his presentation; however, he still respected Coach Charley and Coach Davis. He could not turn down this invitation.

Eric was escorted by his mentors to the top floor of the Wyndham Hotel—to the Executive Presidential Penthouse Apartment Suite by Trump. This house was draped with gold flake on the walls, gold fixtures in the bathrooms and kitchen. There were intricate murals on the walls. The smallest television in the house was a 50" Plasma. Women were running around in all stages of dress from scantily clad to buck-bald-naked. But what caught Eric's attention was the Coaches in attendance.

As the trio walked through the party, Eric noticed it was a real "who's who" among colleges and coaches from all around the country. In one corner stood the Oklahoma group with Barry Switzer and Bob Stoops. In another corner were the Florida boys – Steve Spurrier, Roy Kidd, and Division II legend Frank Cignatti. The Texas group was holding court near the balcony led by Mack Brown, Darrell Royal, David McWilliams, and Will Muschamp.

The room was packed with coaches. The centerpiece of the party was an ice sculpture of the National Championship trophy with Louis XIII pouring from the center. Eric felt the same way he had when he attended his very first convention as a graduate assistant. It was like when he was on the elevator

123

with the legendary coach Eddie Robinson – he felt a sense of accomplishment. Eric knew that he had arrived. It was a strange but good feeling. He almost crapped in his pants when Phil Fulmer from the University of Tennessee, extended a speaking engagement invitation to him. Coach Fulmer indicated that he was intrigued by Eric's scheme and felt that his defensive staff would benefit from a talk with him. To Eric this was an unbelievable honor; he could not believe Coach Fulmer even knew his name.

When Eric and Coach Charley finally got a chance to chat privately, the old man told Eric that he was so proud of him and that he loved him, and that he knew all along that one day the young man would make a great coach.

"Thanks for the compliment, Coach," Eric smiled. "Those words really mean a lot coming from you. But, Coach, you could have hired me when I was there with you."

"You know it wasn't my practice to hire my players," The old man insisted. He'd only ever hired two former players as coaches, and they were players when he was an assistant coach at a Division I school in Alabama.

"Coach, you know times have changed, and you have to change with them."

"I know, and you're right. Maybe one day I will."

Eric asked Coach Charley if he had seen or talked with James. "No, I haven't," the old man replied. "How is he doing at Bankhead?" asked Coach Charley while shaking hands with the Mayor of Houston and the owner of the local NFL team.

"He was let go from Bankhead, but I don't know why." Just as Eric completed his sentence, one wild coach from Arizona State cut loose with one of the ladies in attendance, drinking shots off her exposed navel.

"If you see him, tell him to get in touch with me."

Eric started to tire, so he set off to find his boss. After finding Coach Davis, Eric thanked him for the great time and the opportunity to meet all those great coaches. "I have to go," he said. "I need to prepare and work on my presentation." Looking to his left, Eric noticed the Head Coach of Notre Dame emerging from a room with two women trailing him. His hair was disheveled, shirt half-tucked, and his belt hanging unbuckled. While he laughed, one of the cocktail waitresses perpetually circling the party handed him a Long Island Iced Tea, which he dispatched of speedily.

"Okay," Coach Davis said, "but your presentation isn't for another two days!" Coach Davis was flanked by two women—one with fire red hair and the other a nice Latina bearing a remarkable resemblance to Sofia Vergara. "Son, I've got my hands full and you're gonna just leave like that? I thought that you were a team player!" Eric could hear Coach Davis' hearty drunken laughter as he closed the door while exiting the convention's ode to hedonism.

After Eric got back to his room, he was able to exhale. The first thing he did after regrouping from his eventful night was call his wife. He didn't care that it was two o'clock in the morning. Angela answered the phone very sleepily, "What's wrong, baby?"

"Nothing's wrong," he assured her. "Baby, you won't believe my night! I was invited to where all the big boys go to have a good time. It was unbelievable the coaches who were there! Now I know why you don't see coaches at that level out very much – it's because they have their own fraternity where they're never in public to be bothered by all the coaches looking for jobs."

James had been beating the pavement looking for a job. He'd found that he had become a social outcast to many coaches; he was even going to the job board to see what jobs were available. Not one day passed at the convention that he wasn't wearing a navy-blue blazer and a nice tie like he was destined to make First Team All-Lobby, Second Team All-Airport.

James felt he had hit rock bottom with his search. He had interviewed for a couple of NCAA Division II assistant jobs. He didn't find anything wrong with Division II football, but he was distorted by the fact that just one year ago he had been listed as one of the top ten college football recruiters. He was now hearing all the various reasons that schools couldn't hire him — you're not married, we already hired somebody, we are looking for some other position, etc. Excuse, after excuse, after excuse. No one would accept or return his calls.

Still, he put his problems on hold to be there for his old roommate's presentation at the conference. He arrived at the session room early, just in case he saw someone of importance. When Eric arrived, it was a sight. James felt proud of his old roommate. The two of them had a bond that had been cultivated over many years, as a result of that unfortunate date with a pre-op tranny, long ago. Words could not describe the closeness between the two coaches.

James went over to his friend. "Knock 'em dead!" he grinned.

"Thanks, man". Eric smiled back. "Hey, after this is over, we need to talk."

"Okay." As James prepared to take a seat, he noticed Coach Charley and went over talk to him.

"James," the old man greeted his former player, "how are things going?"

"Not very good, Coach," James replied honestly. "I need a job. Do you know anyone that has an opening?"

Coach Charley said that he did know anyone with an opening and would love to help him, but that James had to be straight with him about what had happened with his last job. This was new territory for James. There were only three people to whom James could confess his sins and not be judged. This trinity included Momma Dear Leaf, Coach Charley, and Eric. If you were thinking that some preacher would be in that three, forget it! The Beast was never big on attending church. In college, James was the classic Easter

Sunday and Christmas Service attendee. I suppose that when you've been C.O.M.W. (Cutting Other Men's Women) since high school, there is a chance you would become indifferent about seeking salvation. Any social psychologist would suggest that James' relationship/marriage wrecking behavior is indicative of some deeply repressed self-loathing that needs to be addressed. James would simply contend that he was "trying girls out— married or not."

Nevertheless, James went through the details for Coach Charley of what happened at Bankhead. In the Beast's classic style, he began his confession with a toast by quoting Wyclef Jean—the playa Haitian from The Fugees fame: "To all the girls I fucked before, to all the girls I've cheated on before." Four mojitos, a bottle of Grey Goose, and one of Lemon Garlic Chicken, and a dish of Lobster & Crab ravioli later, Coach Charley's mind was blown. James did not leave out a single detail. He told Coach Charley that he regretted the whole situation. Coach Charley was stunned particularly that on his recruiting visit, James was part of a double-team gang bang on Alice with Big Derek. James credited that night with Alice as being the catalyst to his commitment to knocking down women who were otherwise "off-limits." He explained that he would change it if he could, but he could not change it now. But somehow for James this situation with Kirsten was different and he told Coach Charley the same.

The old man took everything in stride outwardly, but he was tripping over the fact that James had been cutting his best friend, Alice under his nose— for all Coach Charley knew, James was still sleeping with Alice. Oh yeah, he was, whenever he was back in the Baltimore area, Alice made it a point to get a little bit of beef steak to go with her gravy—He asked one question: "Do you love this woman?" To James' surprise, the first word out of his mouth was "Yes." James had never said it before, but he had come to the realization that he really cared for Kirsten. Moved by the depth of James' confession,

Coach Charley asked if there was a chance for them to which James replied, "No! She's in love with her husband, and she went back to him for the sake of the kids and the time they have spent together and all that other bullshit." This conversation was very cathartic for James, who despite the amount of alcohol consumed to this point remained sober and coherent. For James, this was his moment of clarity. Coach Charley could tell that this situation had broken James; it had forced him to mature and consider the consequences of his reckless actions. James had turned a corner in his life. Perhaps he was ready to make the commitment to his coaching career that Eric had made from the outset.

As the presentation began, James thanked his old coach for listening to him. John Davis introduced Coach Eric Fellows to the audience, telling about how they had met and continued with the growth of their friendship and working relationship. He finished by saying, "It is my honor to present to you, my defensive coordinator at Western Ohio, Coach Eric Fellows".

Eric's presentation was great. He wasn't like most presenters at the conference; he went into great detail about his philosophy, his scheme, and the tactics that he employed. The audience was awed that a coach would actually lay out his scheme. Eric remembered when he came to his first convention how vague the presenters were, and he'd vowed then to be different. After speaking for 40 minutes, he spent the last 20 minutes answering audience questions. As he finished, Coach Fellows was given a standing ovation. James was in awe. He simply couldn't believe how much his friend had grown as a coach. He knew from that moment on that he had to raise his standards from being more than the best recruiter on a staff – he had to be a good coach as well.

After the presentation was over, Coach Charley walked over to James and said, "I have a job for you. My tight end coach and recruiting coordinator is leaving to take a head coaching job at a high school in Miami, Florida. No one knows it yet, but it's your job if you want it."

This seemed odd, knowing what Coach Charley now knew about James and Alice. This fact was not lost on James as well. James looked at his old coach and mentor with tears in his eyes. "Thank you," he said, "I won't let you down, I would be honored to work for you and my alma mater."

"Stay away from the wives! Especially Alice!" Coach Charley joked, but sharply. "I am sure I will get some backlash from the staff for hiring you, but I can handle that." As everyone is leaving, the old man says to Eric, "Great job. It was one of the best presentations I have ever heard at a coaching convention."

After the crowd dwindled, the only people left were Eric, John Davis, and James. "Great job," Coach Davis joked with Eric, "but you could have left something for their imagination." James showed his notebook with twelve pages of notes. Eric was shocked that James took notes, but was flattered that the twelve pages, at a glance, included details that showed that James was listening. To Eric, this was evidence that James was beginning to become serious about the profession of coaching.

"It's nice to see you again, Coach Davis," James said.

"Likewise," John replied as he departed.

James told Eric that he was awesome. "The old man was here and told me to tell you that you were great!"

"Thanks. Coach just told me I did a good job. My adrenaline got going and I couldn't stop!"

"Let's get something to eat. My treat!" said James.

"No, no. You need to save your money. You know you are unemployed."

"True," James smiled, "but that's about to change. You can't tell anybody this, but Coach Charley is going to make me his tight end coach and recruiting coordinator."

Eric stopped cold when he heard this. No matter how much time passed, Eric's skin was as thin as butcher's paper. He took everything adverse as an intentional insult. Coach Charley had told him years ago that he did not hire his former players. Eric couldn't help but think that the old man was saving his golden boy. And after the stunt, he'd pulled at Bankhead, no less! Eric felt betrayed. Still, he managed to tell his friend, "That's great!" James and Eric hugged each other. James thought that he finally had a chance to make things right. While Eric walked away, though, he felt depressed that James was still able to "shine" on his big day.

9 CROSSROAD

To date, Eric had put in the necessary work. He had pounded the pavement at each convention. The necessary contacts were being made; however, Eric's thirst for more was not satisfied. With Angie's help, Eric was becoming more of an optimist, believing his break was just around the corner. On the very day in January that Coach Eric Fellows gave his presentation on defensive football, a subtle gesture by a pair of influential friends, solidified his status as a "rising young coach." Coach Davis and Coach Charley strategically invited Eric to the party so that other head coaches could put a face with his name. They both knew that a coach of Eric's caliber needed a break to move to the next level.

The party itself was different from any Eric had attended to this point. It was more like a mixer than a party. Coaches were simply socializing and chatting with one another. It was akin to being back in the locker room for Eric—in the beaming following a hard fought victory and a hot shower, looking forward to some hot sex on a platter with a delectable young coed. This party was also different in the sense that no scantily clad women were running around. There were at least twenty head coaches in attendance by Eric's informal count. This was a meeting of men that called shots; these were men running programs; these were men that could change your life with a handshake. Interestingly, there were no other coordinators or assistant coaches there. It was just Eric.

Eric would speak with all the head coaches in attendance; however, eleven coaches would pull him aside for impromptu interviews throughout the night. Eric was on his game from the outset. The discussions with each head coach did not center on five-(5) year plans; ideas on turning around moribund programs; touting upcoming recruiting classes; or, any of those typical talking points. Eric was struck by how much these coaches were interested in him as a person and how much that he cared about coaching. Many of the coaches wanted to know about Eric's family life and how he dealt with not playing as much as he would have liked in college. Coach George Campbell from Texas Southern University, an HBCU in Houston, was particularly interested in seeing Eric's mind at work—asking him about religion, the economy, race relations, and where Eric stood on flat tax debate.

Eric could talk football anytime, anyplace, for as long as people would allow, but he now understood that being a great football coach was deeper than just football. For the most part, parents send their sons to colleges for education; however, parents tend to want coaches that can help their sons become well-rounded men—not just great football players. Eric believed that he had made great conversational points in his "interviews." He was mostly pleased with the fact that these coaches saw him as a good man with a sharp mind with fresh ideas but willing to be "coached" himself. He believed that these were qualities that transcended coaching and were applicable to most any career.

That break came soon after when Eric was contacted by Cumberland State University to become the defensive coordinator. Yes, Cum State! I couldn't believe it either. I read about it while getting tape before practice on a Wednesday. It was a headline in the USA Today. I cannot imagine who leaked the story of the offer. Eric had to think about the decision to work at CSU. He was grateful for the opportunity, but he was not getting the same hot-coach-of-the-moment buzz he remembered Coach Fred Davis receiving as the offensive coordinator at State. But he received some buzz just the same.

He decided to decline the offer. He told his friends that he didn't want to work at his alma mater's rival school, but his real reason was that he knew his wife didn't want to move back to a rural area. She really enjoyed being in Cincinnati after all those years living in the middle of nowhere. Eric's friends thought that he must take a coaching opportunity when it presented itself;

they figured if he turned down the Cumberland job, other schools might stop calling. But Eric had a plan. He did not want to be seen as a job-hopper that simply used schools as stepping-stones to other schools. He was the "little-guy" while playing in college and enjoyed coaching for a "little guy." There was something to be said for a consistently well-coached "mid-major" college going from canon-fodder during bowl-season to a legitimate program that was feared by large programs looking to complete schedules in the off-season.

Eric knew that he could be selective in choosing a job because he already had a job – a good job at that. He didn't necessarily need to leave. His defensive unit at Western Ohio was consistently ranked at the very top, but it was Angela who asked him what he wanted from coaching. "If Western Ohio is all that you want, then I'm with you, but if you need something else, I'm with you still." Eric and his wife had come a long way in their relationship. They were the proud parents of Kevin and Erica, and their marriage had really started to flourish once Angela got back to working and developing a life separate from her football coach husband.

When Eric was offered a job at Central Alabama University in the Old South Conference – arguably the best conference in the country – he jumped at the opportunity. Located in Birmingham, Central Alabama was where football was king. Eric figured there was no better place to showcase his talents as a coach than down south. Eric received a call from the legendary Coach Johnny Palmer to take a trip to Alabama and interview for the defensive coordinator position. Eric's intuition alerted him that this would be a good trip.

"Where do you see yourself down the road in coaching," Coach Palmer asked.

"I want your job, Coach," Eric replied. "I want to be a head coach, and I've tried to do all the right things so that one day, I could be sitting in your chair."

"What do you think your role is as a coach?"

Eric thought for a minute, then replied, "To make your job easier, Coach. I want you never to have to worry about the defense; I want you to have faith that we will get the job done."

Coach Palmer stood quietly for a moment. Eric couldn't tell if that was a good or a bad sign since Palmer was one of those old, crusty coaches who showed very little emotion. Finally, the head coach asked, "How does your wife feel about moving to the south?"

"My wife is a college coach's wife. She understands this business and will be very supportive in what I feel is best for our family."

Coach Palmer had one of the young coaches on his staff show Eric around campus. When the tour was over, Eric was brought back to Palmer's spacious office. The head coach looked him in the eye and said, "Son, what do you think? Do you want to be the next defensive coordinator here a CAU?"

"Coach Palmer, it would be my honor," Eric replied with no hesitation. The answer came out so quickly that he never even thought about discussing pay or benefits.

After their meeting, Eric flew back to Cincinnati. While on the plane, Eric realized that Coach Palmer never mentioned what he would have to run on defense, nor did he bring up anything regarding the defensive scheme. He didn't fret nor begin to obsess it. His gut just gave him a sense that Coach Palmer would turn over the keys to the defense to him and provide him with everything that he needed to field a formidable defensive unit. Eric felt so at ease, and he knew Angela would be pleased about his decision.

Back in Baltimore, James felt that the city had really changed since the old days. The last time he was at State, he had been on top of the world. Everybody in the state used to treat "The Beast" like he was larger than life. He was just a face in the crowd now. James knew times had changed. When he went to visit with Coach Charley for the first time, the secretary didn't know who he was, only his name. Gone were the days of Ms. Alice, who had recently retired after 35 years.

James asked the new secretary, "Is Coach Charley in?"

"Yes," Ms. Jamison replied. "And who may I tell Coach Charley is here?"

"James Ryan Leaf," he said smiling widely, expecting the woman to fall to her knees.

"Oh, the new football coach. I'm sorry, but I haven't done your paperwork yet. I didn't know you would be here today."

Not exactly the response James had been expecting. "Well, I'm a day early," he smiled, "but everybody knows me around here."

Looking James up and down, "I guess I missed that memo," responded the secretary flatly.

James was just a coach at his alma mater, and no longer "the legend." It was a rude awakening, but also an amazing confirmation of his maturity because very few people remembered the things that he did as a player. Although it hurt his ego that he was not remembered as an all-time great like Paul Ubeck – a great quarterback in the 70's who went on to play in the NFL, James didn't lash or act out and do something silly. He realized that he was in a different chapter of his life now; he was in a different chapter of his coaching career. He could no longer trade on his former prowess on the field. James knew now that his success or failure as a coach would depend on upon his actions and decisions from this point forward.

Every once in a while, though, someone from James' era would surface and remember the years of "The Beast". It was during these times that James would venture back to his bad behavior of the past, like the time when Eddie Parker came up from D.C. and bumped into him on campus. The two started acting like the kids they were in the old days. Eddie was a good guy, but he still had a lot of bad habits that he'd never given up. In other words, Eddie was still a "hook"—another way of calling a person a crook. He had been a D.C. legend who came to State University as a fullback, but he quit after he was moved to defensive end. He stayed in the Baltimore area and was the campus "Weed Man". The spitting image of comedian Charlie Murphy, Eddie's motto was, "I'll go git it and come back wit it." I can still hear his crazy ass now. Sometimes within an hour before the game, you could hear him, "I can get it whenever you need it." Out the backdoor of the locker room, he would go.

The two old buddies reminisced for hours about the practices, the girls, and the old gang, and wound up in one of the sleaziest strip clubs in B'More– Loose Booty. I mean, this place was in the bottom, down in the gut. Loose Booty featured heavy blunt smoking patrons, watered-down drinks, old ass bouncers, and old ass dancers but the place was so clean—it was classy. There might have been two dancers in there that were easy on the eyes. The others were just wrong for being there. The owner was wrong for having them there. The clowns dropping dollars on them were wrong and drunk, but damn wrong just the same. These were the sort of gals that might have bullet wounds and straight razor scars. I mean these hoes had been through it. They gave you a dance for five dollars and then take you in the back for a quick carnal session for ten more. You'll never see more smoked-out strippers than you will at Loose Booty. In the middle of all this waist deep, was a former legend and current coach for State U.

James and Eddie, of course, had a ball at the club. They continued to reminisce late into that night, until suddenly, the music shut-off. They heard a loud voice say, "Get your hands up!" The police were raiding the club! The fear in James' eyes was undeniable. He could imagine himself on the morning news, caught up in a strip club drug raid! While James was cuffed and placed in the back of a police cruiser, he realized that he had too much to lose from being involved with some of the people from his past. As he prayed, a cop came to the door and uncuffed him.

James recognized the officer; it was Gus Capalano, a former teammate from State. Gus played guard and was a senior during James' freshman year. Following graduation, Gus joined the force. Gus told James to get the hell outta there while escorting him to the backdoor. James wasted no time getting out of Loose Booty.

That was the last time he saw Eddie, and he knew he had barely escaped a nightmare. Eddie has a quarter-ounce of weed and a Llama blue-steel 9mm on him. With that, Eddies' truck was searched. The pigs found a quarter pound of the purple in the stashbox of his Escalade truck next to a chrome .380. He was on bond for Battery on a Police Officer, Possession of Crack with intent to Distribute, and Failure to Appear. There wouldn't be any further bonds for Eddie. The City of B'More seized the truck and his baby mama seized everything else—headed for Florida.

As he drove off, James began crying like a baby. James realized that he needed Coach Charley's influence to help him make better decisions in life.
****

Meanwhile, down south, Eric was in for a real culture shock. Football in Alabama was much different than any other place he had ever coached. The radio and television stations talked about the Central Alabama Tigers twenty-four hours a day. Eric knew he was in the big leagues when, at his first spring game, there were more than 68,000 people in the stadium, and the television and radio stations wanted to interview him after the game.

Spring games are generally fairly pedestrian. Conventional wisdom is that defenses have an advantage in the spring; but, this game was different.

The CAU offense boasts 20 lettermen including 9 starters. The only two losses were to the NFL. The offensive line featured eight juniors and 2 seniors. The quarterback was a fifth-year senior and conference player of the year candidate. This offense averaged 42 points per game for the last two years. Literally, when this offense hits the field, six touchdowns will be scored. Eric's defense, on the other hand, was led by a core group of 6 redshirt sophomores in the front seven with 4 freshmen in the secondary. These facts provided all the trappings for an offensive explosion in the spring game. The opposite took place. Eric's base scheme featured three fronts and four coverages. Eric pressured the quarterback with at least five players on each snap. Those kids were simply flying around the field making plays and Eric was just as excited as if he was in the game. The first team offense scored three field goals. No touchdowns were scored against the first team defense.

Eric had reached the level in his career that he had hoped for when he started out. However, once he got there, things weren't right. After the first season ended, Eric always seemed to be down. He had a lot to be thankful for – he now coached a team that played in a New Year's Day Bowl and finished the season with Top 10 rankings – but every day he felt a weight on his shoulders from working in such a successful program. Angela began to notice the uneasiness in her husband. Every day she would ask him if everything was okay, and he would always lie and say that everything was great.

Eric noticed that the staff at Central Alabama was not very close, and this was one thing that he really missed from Western Ohio. Coach Miller, Coach Traylor and Coach Denson were all great guys to work with on the defensive staff, but they treated Eric like a boss and not a colleague. The defensive staff knew Coach Palmer didn't mind firing employees, and this kept the staff on pins and needles. No one wanted to get to know each other; they just wanted to keep their own jobs secure.

Coaching at Central Alabama was pure business. Coach Palmer was concerned with touchdowns and not giving up touchdowns. Show him an injury report and he'll show you kids looking to skip practice. Try to explain a weakness of a play design against a particular front/coverage combination and Coach Palmer will lecture you on the merits of execution. For the offensive coaches, Coach Palmer simply wanted to see that scoreboard ringing. It was their job to get it done. He didn't want to be buried with if-then scenarios; Coach Palmer wanted the facts and HE would make the decisions. A familiar mantra of Coach Palmer—to coaches and players alike—was "you let me do all the thinking." It was a conundrum for Eric. Yeah, I know. I used conundrum, I have to do something with my degree—in Communications. Nevertheless, Eric is having problems dealing.

Coach Palmer was an enigma. There were not many "atta-boys" coming from him. In fact, Coach Palmer has turned out to be quite the curmudgeon in coaches meetings. Perhaps none of the coaches truly knew of the pressure being applied on Coach Palmer by the University President and the alumni. These people were rabid, fanatical, uncompromising carnivores. Thus, "CP" as he was affectionately known to his friends, morphed from a coach into a result-oriented corporate manager. All he wanted was results and didn't care about obstacles, problems, and concerns. The interesting aspect of all this pressure applied by Coach Palmer is that it created an environment of innovation. Several former offensive coordinators had moved on to head coaching jobs. His defensive coordinators did not fare as well. Until Eric.

To deal with the pressures of his job, Eric started to drink heavily. It was not unusual for him to consume a case of beer at the office while breaking down film, and then another six-pack when he got home. Angela tried unsuccessfully to convince him to stop drinking so much. Finally, she conceded but asked her husband not to drive home if he'd been drinking. Eric would always tell his wife, "I'm fine! I know when I've had too much!"

It was during one of his bouts of binge drinking and film study that Eric made the discovery that would distinguish him at CAU. So many college defensive ends were being converted to linebackers to combat the wide-open pass happy offenses of the day. Eric decided to make the conversions now. He converted the defensive philosophy of Coach Jerry Tarkanian, a noted college basketball coach, and applied it to football. Coach Tarkanian called his defense "The Amoeba." Eric named his defense "The Raptor." It was reminiscent of Buddy Ryan's "46" defense popularized by the Chicago Bears. In essence, "The Raptor" consisted of 3 defensive backs and 6 linebackers. This was essentially a personnel package that he developed at Western Ohio. It proved to be very effective on 3rd down. CAU was blessed with very athletic players; many were hybrids that could play more than one position. Coach Palmer was fond of pulling potential recruits off basketball courts and projecting them into various positions. Eric now saw what his schemes could accomplish with this group of players. His career would never be the same if he could just keep it all together. Ninety-nine bottles of beer on the wall and counting, you know how it goes.

Three years, three huge bowl appearances, three victories including a 28-0 shutout of Ohio State in the Fiesta Bowl, and one Top-5 finish. Yet, Eric continued to drink. He was not enjoying the success that he worked so hard to achieve. Desperate to reach her husband to get him out of his funk, Angela decided that she would throw Eric a surprise party. He had won the Defensive Coordinator of the Year Award, so Angela went out of her way to make this party the best ever. She invited former players, teammates, coaches, and family. This was a celebratory surprise party. James was there with Angela every step of the way, helping to put the party together for the most deserving man – a husband, a friend, and a great coach.

James had really made a life change after the raid at Loose Booty. He became involved with a church and was an active member of the Fellowship of Christian Athletes. Before the raid, he would just go to FCA events when they were mandatory, or when they had something to eat, but now he was participating fully in the organization. He also got engaged to a beautiful young lady that he'd met in church, Lisa Chambers. He and Lisa had dated for over a year, and she was the best thing that could have happened to him.

It was a beautiful night at the party Angela planned. Eric could not believe all the people that came to honor him. Even Alice, Coach Charley's long-time secretary, showed up to celebrate. After the initial surprise and some festivities, people started yelling to Eric, "Speech! Speech!"

"Everyone here is a part of what I have become," Eric said as he stood up in front of his family and friends, "and I love each and every one of you." He couldn't help breaking into tears, crying to see all the people that loved him. It was such an emotional day for Eric, and all he could think of was the long, difficult journey it had taken for him to become the top defensive coordinator in the country.

Angela wanted everyone to be involved with the party, even the kids. She knew that her children, Kevin and Erica, had grown up as coach's kids, and they were a big part of Eric's success. Kevin, especially, was a great kid who loved to joke and entertain. He was the one who would show off the latest dance steps or songs for his parents and their friends. During the party, Kevin started showing off for some of the other kids who were attending the party. He joked around, playing near the street, but not exactly in the street. He just wanted the other kids to have a good time.

Suddenly, out of nowhere, a car sped down the street and hit Kevin as he barely stepped off the curb. The scene was horrifying. The other kids screamed and cried hysterically as the adults came running out of the house. James' fiancée Lisa, who was a nurse, performed first aid and CPR on Kevin before the paramedics arrived. Her efforts did no good, and by the time the paramedics made it to the scene, it was too late. His little body lay motionless. Kevin was pronounced died on the scene; he had been hit and killed by a drunk driver.

The next season was an extremely long one for the Fellows family. Eric blamed himself for his son's death and began to doubt many of the decisions he had made. He blamed everything on his move from Cincinnati. Angela was the glue that held the family together. Little Kevin had been her pride and joy, but she knew that her son would have wanted his family to keep living their lives to the fullest. At least that is what mourners say to themselves to ease their own grief. For all we know, Little Kevin may have wanted his family to suffer for having not scolded him in the past for playing near and in the street. Perhaps he would have simply been playing in the yard instead of dancing near the curb.

In any event, Lil' Kevin was a bundle of energy. He was very active with Eric during game preparations. Angela used to love watching the two of them review game film together. Kevin had progressed to the point where he recognized unbalanced lines, route combinations, and understood the reasoning behind "stemming" a defensive front. "Stemming" is basically shifting from one front to another just prior to the snap of the ball. Kevin was so inquisitive. He asked a lot of questions of everyone he met. Coach Palmer was fond of Kevin and loved seeing him running around the Coaches offices. Kevin had lived the ten short years of his life as freely as possible. He was always pulling practical jokes and clowning around to make everyone feel good.

James knew that his friend needed him now more than ever. It was remarkable how James responded. He was great at being there for his friend. It was during this time that James and Eric revisited a past ritual – the early morning wake up calls to one another. This was a wonderful, healing therapy for them. James and Eric found that they were both at a crossroads in life, and they needed to find a way to keep going forward.

10 SCORE

The human condition is ripe for repetition. Oftentimes, the response to a traumatic event is one of introspection. There are no hard and fast rules to mourning. Eric and Angela were dealing with the death of their son in their own way. Eric was amazed that two weeks after Kevin's death, the local sports talk radio show was still abuzz regarding the upcoming football season. It appeared that the fans of Central Alabama were simply oblivious to the Fellows' family's pain. Yet, three months after the funeral, Angela started a business consulting firm. Additionally, she voiced her interest in having another child—which disgusted Eric who was enduring an emotional roller-coaster. Eric was desperate for a closer relationship with his coaching comrades. Yet, the coaching staff would never be close. Closeness was not conducive to the winning and it was not part of the culture at Central Alabama. Training camp was fast approaching, but Eric no longer had the drive. With that, he told Angela he couldn't do it anymore. He had had enough.

Shocked, Angela asked her husband, "Is it coaching that you're tired of, or is it coaching in Alabama?" Furthermore, Angela made it clear that she did not want Eric crawling into a shell following Kevin's death. "I don't want you using my son's death as some sort of crutch to avoid facing the obstacles in your life."

"Coaching in Alabama, baby. I am tired of this place." Eric said, "But I could let it all go." Angela continued to call Eric to task. "I think that's a load of shit. We didn't raise Kevin to be a coward and I didn't marry one." Eric stood up. He was noticeably upset with Angela's tone.

"Baby, I mean no disrespect. But you need to hear this. If you have problems with the way things are going at CAU, then change it…from the ground up." Eric couldn't believe his ears. His wife had finally gone mad.

Eric had no authority at CAU to effect the changes that he felt were necessary to win a national title. The talent was on campus and the coaches were energetic, intelligent, and great tacticians—but there was no commitment. It was always one eye on the game plan, one eye on the door. "It just doesn't happen, Eric. You've gotta make it happen."

Eric knew that he and the family needed a change of scenery and that if an opportunity for a new job came about, he would probably take it. Over the previous couple of years, people had been calling to hire him. But he didn't feel that they were good jobs – they were lateral moves or demotions.

"Would you accept one of the Division I-A or I-AA head coaching jobs that are open?" Angela asked.

"Yeah," Eric replied, "if it meant leaving Birmingham."

***

Angela knew her husband was depressed, but it was coaching that had given him the will to move forward. One day, Angela called James to ask him how she could handle the situation with Eric.

"Angela, give me a couple of days," James told her, "and I think I can give you some advice for relief. Does Eric know you still talk to me?"

"No, he doesn't know. But you know that I could never just cut you totally out of our lives." In the past, James might have pounced on such a "hungry" comment. Those days were long behind him now. In his newfound spirituality, James went to the person that he respected most – his mentor, Coach Charley. After four seasons with old man Charley, their relationship had blossomed into a father-son bond. It was something James never experienced as a player because he was the star and had derived his fulfillment from the outside world. At that point in life, Coach Charley could not have given him what he gave players now or even the coaches. Coach Charley had become a father figure to the team and had long since taken his hands out of the day-to-day operations of the team.

145

One day after meeting with the old man about recruiting, James talked about the problems Eric was having at CAU. He said that Eric was contemplating giving up his coaching career. Coach Charley knew deep down in his heart that this was a mistake, but he told James that everyone must fight their own demons and that everything would clear itself out for Eric. The Lord has a plan for him just as He has a plan for us all.

"I may retire in the next week or two," the old man continued, throwing James totally off-guard. "My time here is almost over. I've been coaching now for over 40 years and my health is starting to become an issue. And I want to spend more time with my family." Stunned, James says, "Coach, I know you're kidding!" James replied, still in shock. Continuing, James said, "Right? I mean, you have more to give to these athletes, and you know it."

"Thanks for the compliment, but if you read the Baltimore Newspapers, you would realize you're in the minority for thinking that."

James knew the fans at State University had been calling for Coach Charley's job for over 10 years now. State hadn't been to a New Year's Day Bowl in over 12 years and hadn't been ranked in the Top 10 in six years. The public cried out for the old man's job since they knew his best days were behind him. Still, Coach Charley was a legacy. "You are State University!" he insisted. The old man was flattered, but he knew that football would survive without him. He was not sure, however, that he could survive without football.

James knew that this was the job for Eric, but he didn't know how to make it work. Ironically, James had always wanted to be the next head coach at State, but he realized he could never get the job. He hadn't prepared himself for that day, and he didn't command respect as a coach to give State University what they wanted. But Eric did.

Two days after the call from Angela, James called her back. He never said anything about Coach Charley retiring, but told Angela, "Keep Eric's spirits up. I have something in the works that would keep him excited for the next 20 years. I need you to just work with me!"

Coach Charley wanted to announce his retirement after the national signing day. As the national letters of intent were being returned to the office, James was able to get Coach Charley alone to talk more about his possible retirement.

"Do you have a successor for the job?" he asked. Everyone had just assumed over the years that Coach Charley's long-time defensive coordinator Ronald Thompson would become the next head coach at State University. But James knew that with the decline in the program that State needed a spark and was going to go in another direction.

Coach Charley replied, "No, I don't have a successor. I was going to tell the athletic director to do what he felt was best for the program. But James, I don't think they could justify hiring you, especially after the raid at that strip club."

James was shocked that Coach Charley knew about the incident because he had never told anyone about that incident. "I'm sorry about that, Coach," he said, "but I didn't want to embarrass you and the program."

"I know. You were lucky that one of the cops at the scene was a former player of mine and knew who you were."

"But coach, I'm talking about Eric Fellows. This is the job he was born to have. He's worked his way up the ranks to become one of the best coordinators in the country. Eric can continue your legacy." Coach Charley asked James if Eric had put him up to this. "Coach, I haven't told anyone about your intentions because I still don't believe you'll retire." The old man told James to let him think about his recommendation before he put his name on the line to endorse a successor.

During one of their early morning rituals, James asked Eric, "What head coaching job would you want most?"

"You know I want to coach at State," Eric sighed, "but the last time I talked to the old man, he said he was sure he was going to do at least five more years. I can't wait that long. I would've already gotten a job or tried to get into the pros by the time he came through."

"Yeah, I know. I was just checking to see if you had changed your mind." James asked his friend one last question, "If you got that head job, say, at another school, who would be your offensive coordinator?"

Eric took a long pause, which put James on edge. Finally, he said, "You know it's you, man! You know, in the end, there is nobody I trust more than you."

James knew he really had to work Coach Charley, so that night, he stopped by the old man's house.

"So, Coach, have you thought about the successor question?"

"Yes," Coach Charley replied. "I have," He had been thinking of Eric ever since he started contemplating retirement, but he had to see what the athletic director was thinking. He tells James that he would help Eric in any way he could. "But don't tell Eric about this conversation," he said. "This is the athletic director's call."

The next day, when the Fellows family made it home from dinner, Angela checked their voicemail. One of the messages that was left went: "Coach Eric Fellows, this is Mrs. Marie Taylor, Athletic Director of Maryland State University in Baltimore, Maryland. When you receive this message, please call me on my cell phone at 410-777-6969."

"Eric!" Angela shouted to her husband. "Come quick! Listen to this message!" Eric listened to the message, then shrugged. "It's probably an alumni function going on." He waited until the next morning to return Mrs. Taylor's call. When the athletic director answered, her voice was quick and direct, like Condoleezza Rice.

"Coach Charley will retire at the end of this week," Mrs. Taylor stated. "And he has recommended you for his job. I have a lot of respect for Coach Charley, so his recommendation carries a lot of weight with me. If you are interested, let me know now, because this will move fast when it happens. State law requires that I interview three candidates, so I want to know if you would be one."

"Yes," Eric replied after Mrs. Taylor finished. "I would like to be interviewed. But I want to say one thing: Maryland State University is my alma mater. I love it, but if this is just something to keep an alumnus happy, then I don't want to be involved. If you are serious about this and really want me, I'm the man for the job."

"Coach Fellows, I'm making this decision and no one else. I appreciate your honesty, and I will be in touch."

Just as Mrs. Taylor had explained, Coach Charley retired on that Friday. In his retirement speech, he made a reference to his successor. He said that he hoped the next head coach would love Maryland State University as much as he did.

Eric knew that he had to have everything in place to sell Mrs. Taylor. He went into overdrive trying to put together a staff – he called former coworkers, graduate assistants, and friends. He wanted to have a staff ready to present at his interview. He had only one chance at this job, and he was bound and determined not to mess it up. James was also working tirelessly to get the alumni association and other coaches to back Coach Eric Fellows.

During his interview, the athletic director asked him, "What do you need in order to be successful here?"

"Trust," Eric replied simply. "Trust in my decisions. If we have that, then we can work with any constraints that we may have." Mrs. Taylor respected that response since all the other committee members had talked about how they couldn't win without the funding, etc. She felt those other responses had been built on excuses.

Mrs. Taylor then asked Eric if he had any questions. "If you want me to be your head coach," Eric said, "tell me what you want from me. Don't hide behind other people. Be direct and give me the open door to your office to get things done." The athletic director looked at him with a smile; she knew she had her man.

"Coach Fellows," she said, "let's make history. I will start working on the contract immediately."

One week after Coach Charley retired, Eric's dream finally was realized. At the press conference, Marie Taylor announced the next head coach of Maryland State University, alumnus Eric Fellows. It was a proud moment for Eric, as he stood there with his wife and daughter at his side, all of them dressed in their Sunday's best.

Eric paused for a minute and began to speak, "This is the journey I had to take to get to this moment – a personal tragedy, many disappointments, and much rejection. I want to thank my wife, Angela; my daughter, Erica; and my late son, Kevin; for their support. I know that you, State University, won't be disappointed in the product we will put out on the field."

In the audience, there was someone more proud than Eric – his friend James. James couldn't hold back his emotion, as head coach Eric Fellows announced his second hire, offensive coordinator James Ryan Leaf.

Let me tell you about Eric's first hire, Danny Boy. Who? There was no press conference, press release, nor any fanfare whatsoever. Hell, there was no interview. What? Eric didn't talk to Angela about it nor seek the advice of anyone. What took place was two old buds strolling around campus and reminiscing about the days when life was simple. Daniel Boyd or "Danny Boy" as he was commonly called was a very quiet person to most outsiders;

actually, he was considered shy by everyone. Danny Boy, now thirty-eight years old is an institution at State U.

As Eric and Danny Boy continued to walk and talk, passersby would invariably acknowledge Danny Boy before greeting the new football coach. There were several people who knew Danny Boy but had no idea as to the "guy" standing next to him. Everyone that knows Eric loves him. There are no people that have come in contact with Danny Boy that have left disliking or having anything bad to say about him. He is a magnetic figure and passionate about all things associated with State U and for whatever reason Puerto Rican coeds from Texas too. Despite his limitations, Danny Boy breaks convention because, in his own way, he is a very social person such that he initiates interaction in group settings. This facet of his personality accentuates his intelligence.

"Do you still love State U, Danny Boy?" asked Eric. Danny Boy nodded in the affirmative as a young coed stopped to hug him while her friend snapped a picture. "Quick, upload it to Facebook. That was Danny Boy. Can you believe it? I mean, seriously? I'm just a freshman!" said, the young lady as she went on her way. At State U, Danny Boy was a rock star. "I can see that State U. loves you, too." Eric continued on to explain what was happening at State U. Meanwhile, Danny Boy would occasionally nod or audibly in his deep raspy voice respond, "Yep!" Eric couldn't get past the hug. Danny Boy "had come a long way" since Eric's playing days. At that time, Danny Boy did not like to be touched. You would not see him get really agitated; however, you could tell that he was not fond of people that were "hands on." So, to now see Danny Boy welcome an embrace was something of a miracle. Most importantly, it was a testament to his proactive nature and his family's support.

It did not surprise Eric that Danny Boy had an idea about the changes taking place. "Danny Boy will have to leave." Eric became emotional internally at the notion of Danny Boy thinking that he would no longer have a place at State U. Perhaps Danny Boy didn't know that Eric was the new head coach. Sure, there had been no formal announcement, but Danny Boy was never in the dark, at least that's what Eric thought. Eric was shaken from these thoughts and feelings by that simple word from Danny Boy

"Yep," said Danny Boy to Eric's amazement.

Not only did Danny Boy know that Eric was the new coach, but in his own confident way, he knew that Eric had not summoned him for a walk for idle chit-chat. In response, Eric asked the question, a la Alex Tribec and Jeopardy, "What is 'Danny Boy will you stay on with me in your present job?" Eric smiled as Danny Boy reached out to hug him.

The significance of this hire, or rather say holdover, is that Danny Boy is autistic. It was a mystery to what Danny Boy's job or title was at State U. Did Danny Boy go to school at State? Like any unacknowledged elephant in the room, no one even seemed to really care what he did; everyone loved and adored the frumpy cap wearing Danny Boy. The word was that Danny Boy's parents, a wealthy and respected banker from a nearby small town, paid all his expenses. That's right all expenses from his salary to be around the coaching staff, his travel expenses with the team, his bachelor pad, his ride, everything. It was often wondered why no one ever called him "Coach" and not just Danny Boy. Come to find out later that hardly anyone even knew Danny Boy's given name. It was like they really didn't care, he was to them just Danny Boy. He was bigger than State U's president. By the way, who is the President at State? Danny Boy gave everyone he encountered the gift of joy. From an early age, his parents knew that there was something special about Danny Boy He would sit alone sometimes for hours, but was very active. He would socialize in the sense of interacting with others, just without speaking. Thus, upon confirming the diagnosis, Danny Boy's family worked hard to encourage his socializing. What helped him throughout life and at

State U. was a regimented schedule. This is how he came to find out about Eric's becoming head coach. You can generally set your watch by Danny Boy. As fate would have it, Danny Boy was leaving the President's Office as Eric and the Athletic Director walked in on that fateful day. Yeah, Danny Boy knew the time.

What other explanation could there be for Eric and the Athletic Director have for going to see the President?

Coach Charley was fond of Danny Boy after having been introduced to him by his parents after a post-season alumni function. Having been immediately taken by Danny Boy's love for State U., Coach Charley thought it only fitting to figure out a way to make Danny Boy part of the program. Coach Charley never voiced his arrangement with Danny Boy. He researched autism and with the counsel of some trusted State U. faculty, thought it best to have Danny Boy work within the State U. equipment room. Coach Charley thought the benefit of this positioning of Danny Boy was two-fold, first: Danny Boy would have the structured environment that he needed to thrive; and, second: the players would be exposed to Danny Boy, learn his story, and perhaps learn something about dealing with persons with disabilities. Coach Charley also wanted to keep Danny Boy from harm; he didn't allow him on the sideline on game day.

So that's how the legend of Danny Boy started at State U. Danny Boy worked in the equipment room, got to meet and greet the players representing the university that he loved. Danny Boy was very good at special projects like running errands. Over time, he was allowed to assist in the preparations and cleaning of the team uniforms. One year, Danny Boy and Coach Charley started what would become a tradition. One Monday morning Coach Charley arrived for breakfast. Danny Boy was excited because State had just defeated San Mateo Tech by ten. With the assistance of Miss Mattie, the head cafeteria cook, Danny Boy was allowed to present Coach Charley with a custom omelet that had the number ten-(10) made with black olives and bell peppers. That same morning, Danny Boy made a point of getting Miss Mattie to make a special individual plate of fried potatoes and sausage for John Manning, who had just scored three touchdowns and rushed for a then school-record seven rushing touchdowns in a shootout. Coach Charley thought it would be great to have a "Danny Boy Player of the Week" award. The player of the week would be revealed during the time when Danny Boy presented the special breakfast the Monday morning following the game. The players quietly relished the recognition of the special breakfast. Danny Boy was truly a devoted fan of all things State U.

In Eric's mind, as much as anything associated with State U., Danny Boy was vitally important. He needed to remain associated, not only with the university but also with the team. The players considered him one of them in a sense. Eric was considering Danny Boy for a promotion of sorts. Eric wanted him working closer with the players in a dual duty. The Danny Boy Player of the Week tradition would continue; but, Danny Boy would also work with the football operations coordinator as a personal assistant to the head coach of sort. So, this is what Danny Boy did? This would get Danny Boy closer to the team every day, and Eric's right-hand man. Actually, Danny Boy would now be on the sideline on game day with the players for his favorite university. This was Eric's gift to Danny Boy for his years of devoted adulation for State U. Danny Boy would, for his safety, be responsible for the Gatorade table during the game. Eric knew that he would love being on the field, but wanted to make sure that he wouldn't overwhelm Danny Boy

Looking back at the excitement with which Danny Boy accepted the job before it was offered confirmed in Eric that his first hire was the most significant of his young coaching career. Coaching most often is about relationships and loyalty. In this case, Danny Boy's loyalty to the university was a factor but not the factor in his remaining with State U. during Eric's tenure.

****

Several months passed, and it was the final game of the year, and the biggest. The State University Bison were playing their rivals from Cumberland State University – the bunch of fucking assholes from the hills of Maryland. Coach Eric Fellows, the first-year head coach for State, was "Mr. Everything" in turning the football program around.

However, it was a bittersweet day for Coach Fellows. It was the anniversary of his son's death and the university's first invitation to a New Year's Bowl game in over 10 years.

Coach Fellows marveled at how his assistant head coach and offensive coordinator masterfully ripped a new asshole in the assholes from Cumberland. It was ironic to see Coach James "The Beast" Ryan Leaf instructing and mentoring the two young graduate student coaches on trust, character, and responsibility. The young men were all eyes and ears, learning from the engineer of the number one offensive unit in all college football.

Eric Fellows and James Leaf, the two inseparable coaching friends, were now guiding others through their real-life journey in coaching. The two friends felt like they were a touchdown Scoring Drive as their journey toward coaching success was finally accomplished.

About the Authors

After a stellar college playing and coaching career, *Dr. Keith "Mac" McKelphin* is currently the Campus Coordinator at Montgomery College, Germantown Campus. He has been involved for over 18 years at several Colleges and Universities working in the capacity of instructor, strength and conditioning specialist, and as a Coach. Mac worked hard to earn an Ed.D. in Educational Leadership with an emphasis in higher education administration from Liberty University. He earned a M.ED. in Health and Physical Education from Delta State University in 1996, and earned a BS from the University of Southern Mississippi in 1992. Mac is certified by the National Strength and Conditioning Association (NSCA) as a Certified Strength and Conditioning Specialists (CSCSs). In addition, he is a licensed K-12 school teacher. Mac is committed his community service work, so that every student who needs an opportunity to succeed can to achieve their athletic, academic, and professional dreams. Dr. Keith "Mac" McKelphin resides in Maryland, with his wife, Camille, and family.

Ron "Clump" Taylor experienced extraordinary success on the football field as a player and coach, he has become very successful in other business pursuits having honed his consulting expertise in Organizational Dynamics and Records Information Management and Analytics and established his own consulting business through his companies TW Eagle, LLC, and Engagement Solutions, LLC. Clump is committed to ensuring, in his community service work, that every child who wants an education can find a way to access the resources necessary to achieve their academic and professional goals. He is an avid tutor and mentor to middle and high school students. Clump is an author having published a children's book, The Bee Buddies, in 2008. He is also the producer and co-director of the 2010 short film, The Spiral. Ron "Clump" Taylor resides in Oklahoma, with his wife, Yolanda, and family.

www.ingramcontent.com/pod-product-compliance
Lightning Source LLC
Chambersburg PA
CBHW070044260626
47159CB00005B/2119